lady: My Life as a Bitch

★ "Burgess . . . gives teens much to think about in this bawdy, sophisticated, and occasionally sexually explicit adventure, with a host of well-drawn, unusual characters."　　—*Booklist*, starred review

★ "This is a study of human teenage psychology through a dog's snout. . . . Each scene vibrates with verisimilitude."
　　　　　　　　　—*Kirkus Reviews*, starred review

"Burgess is a fearless writer. . . . This seductive volume is as raw and ravenous as its subject."
　　　　　　　　　　　　　—*Publishers Weekly*

The GHOST BEHIND The WALL

Melvin Burgess

THE GHOST BEHIND THE WALL

Henry Holt and Company
New York

Henry Holt and Company, LLC
Publishers since 1866
115 West 18th Street
New York, New York 10011
www.henryholt.com

Henry Holt is a registered trademark of
Henry Holt and Company, LLC.
First published in the United States in 2003
by Henry Holt and Company, LLC.
Distributed in Canada by H. B. Fenn and Company Ltd.
Originally published in Great Britain in 2000
by Andersen Press Limited.

Library of Congress Cataloging-in-Publication Data
Burgess, Melvin.
The ghost behind the wall / Melvin Burgess.
p.   cm.
Summary: Twelve-year-old David sneaks through the ventilation shafts
in his London apartment building pulling pranks on his neighbors, which
awakens the ghost of a boy with a grudge against the lonely, senile old man
who lives upstairs.
[1. Ghosts—Fiction. 2. Memory—Fiction. 3. Old age—Fiction.
4. Apartment houses—Fiction. 5. London (England)—Fiction.
6. Great Britain—Fiction.] I. Title.
PZ7.B9166 Gh 2003   [Fic]—dc 21   2002068806

ISBN 0-8050-7149-0
First American Edition—2003
Designed by Amelia Lau Carling
Printed in the United States of America on acid-free paper. ∞
1   3   5   7   9   10   8   6   4   2

For

Eileen, Bill, Chloë, Annie, and Emily

Contents

The GHOST
BEHIND
The WALL

1

Mahogany Villas

His name was David and he was a bit of a brute, a tough. He was only four foot nothing and twelve years old. His other names were Bum Wipe, Half-boy, and Shorty. He usually ignored it, but once in a while he went mad and nearly killed someone.

He lived with his dad in a high, wide, redbrick building called Mahogany Villas. This building was ten stories high and you got up and down in a clanking elevator with brass doors. The long halls were painted cream and brown and floored with worn, dull, green vinyl tiles. It smelt of cigars and polish and it was the last place you'd think to find a ghost.

The day David discovered you could get behind the walls was a Tuesday after school, when his dad worked late.

He was on a chair in the living room, watching TV, when something fell into the room. It was only a scrap of paper. It came from behind him and landed on the carpet; he caught it out of the corner of his eye. It scared him, because where did it come from? When he looked around, there was no one there. The only thing he could see was the ventilation grille screwed onto the wall.

David stared at this grille. He'd never even thought about it before; it was just there. Now he wondered about it. Where did it go? What was *in* there?

He pushed the sofa up against the wall and climbed up to have a look. It was dark in there, pitch black, and he knew at once that it was big enough for him to get inside if he wanted to. Of course, he didn't want to. Why should anyone want to go creeping about like a rat in the intestines of the old building? But he was glad that grille was screwed into the wall so tightly, that was for sure, because that meant he couldn't get in even if he did want to. Then, to his horror, David saw that the grille wasn't screwed on at all. It was only the metal frame that held the grille that was screwed on. The grille itself was slid sideways into the frame.

4

David pushed the grille; it slid sideways with a sudden jerk and there he was, gazing into the dark heart of Mahogany Villas. His heart twisted and sank. He knew he was going to have to go in there.

It was always like that with David. If it was dangerous, he had to do it. For example, if he had some new toy that he liked very much, he used to hold it as loosely as he could between his fingers and dangle it out of the window. He lived on the fourth floor. Then he'd let his grip get lighter and lighter. He didn't want to let go. The idea was that as soon as the thing slipped, he'd close his fingers and catch it. Mostly he did, but once in a while the thing would slip and be gone—off into the great drop all the way down to the ground.

He'd lost a lot of toys like that. He did it in the car, too—held his favorite things out of the window in the rush of air, just up to the point where the wind would rip them off him and throw them away. He'd done it to plastic fighting men, books, computer games, money, photographs of his mother, marbles, mugs, his dad's glasses. But he'd never done it with his life before. . . .

That thought shocked him. His life? It wasn't that dangerous in there—was it?

"It's just metal tubes," he told himself. They had once been used for air-conditioning, but that hadn't worked for years. Why should the ventilation system hurt him? But then, who knew what was in there? There might be pits to fall in, sharp jags of metal, anything. He could get stuck and starve to death. But that wasn't his real fear. The real reason was that David was certain the ducts were haunted.

As he stood there on the back of the sofa, staring into the dusty, greasy darkness, he could just imagine a cold, whispery voice snaking its way through the ducts toward him. It was a voice made of cobwebs, darkness, dust, and fear, and it was speaking to him.

"Come inside," the voice was saying. "It's dreadful in here. Come on in! You're not scared, are you? You soon will be. . . ."

David imagined the ghost of Mahogany Villas rising up from the lowest pits of the system, filling up the ducts like water, rising higher, higher, until it began to creep along his duct to where he now stood.

He shook his head. This was ridiculous! It was just dark, that's all. But it was very dark, and it was the very scariest kind of dark, too.

"I'm not scared," whispered David to himself.

He got down from the sofa and went to the kitchen to get the flashlight from the drawer. Then he climbed back up to the duct and shone the light inside. All he could see was dust and the joints of the lengths of tube. No voices, no ghosts. He was still scared. He climbed inside.

The dust in there was sticky—not nice. But it was better with the light on. He thought—just as long as he didn't go too far. Just as long as he kept sight of the square of light behind him that opened up into his own safe apartment.

He crawled a little farther in on his elbows. It was scary, but it was good as well. It was so secret. He paused a moment with just his feet sticking out into the living room, before he wriggled one more time and disappeared entirely into the wall.

At least nothing could creep up and get him from behind—not from his own apartment!

David wriggled on, another foot, then a bit more, then a bit more and the floor beneath him suddenly ended and he was staring down a pit, a terrifying pit that plunged down into an unearthly, bottomless darkness. He could so easily have fallen down! It was another duct, bigger than the one he was in. It tipped straight down farther than his flashlight could reach. He gulped and tingled all over with fear. The drop made him sick, but he couldn't help himself. He took the flashlight between his fingers and dangled it over the edge. He let his grip go loose. The flashlight swung in between his fingers. How horrible it would be to have no light!

His grip grew weaker . . . weaker. . . . Then he shook his head and lifted the flashlight out before it slipped between his fingers.

Below him, the duct plunged down to the basement, and above him it went on up to the other six floors of Mahogany Villas. To each side, two more ducts branched off. They were running to the other apartments on the fourth floor. That meant that the ducts could take him anywhere he wanted to go in Mahogany Villas. He could go into other people's apartments. He could steal things. He was a thief in the darkness. He could listen to everything they said. He could spy. He could go through all their most private things.

"My secret," whispered David to himself in a ghostly voice. "*My* darkness. My power," he said aloud. To have power! How nice to have the little people of Mahogany Villas in the palm of his hand!

In a sudden fit of fear, David began to push himself as fast as he could backward out of the ducts. He couldn't even turn around. He shoved and pushed until his legs came out, then with one great heave, he fell feetfirst out of the greasy duct and onto the sofa beneath him. Horrible! That place made him want to shudder. He rolled off the sofa, leaving black marks all over it from the filth he had got on him. He had to go and wash his hands and clean everything up in time for when his dad came back.

David's mother had left him and his dad, Terry, years ago. She'd been offered a job by a cousin of hers in South Carolina, USA. When she first went out there, there were plans for David and his dad to follow on in a month or two when things settled down. They were both looking forward to it, but she kept putting them off and putting them off. First she couldn't find a place for them all to live, then she lost her job and had to get a new one. Then one day she revealed that she'd fallen in love with someone else and didn't want to live with Terry anymore.

  She still wanted David with her, though, and he wanted to go. But his dad wouldn't let him. South Carolina was so far away that you could hardly ever see each other anymore. He was furious with his dad for not letting him go, but he was even more furious with his mother for deserting him. She could come back and get him! She could come home again if she wanted, and she would have if she wanted him badly enough. Her name was Topsy, and she sent him a parcel of clothes and toys and American money three or four times a year.

His dad, Terry, was an optician. When people asked him why he never got married again, he always joked that he was too ugly, but that he was working on a secret pair of glasses, rose-tinted glasses, that would make anyone who wore them fall in love with him at once.

"Then I can have my pick," he used to say, and he'd smack his lips as if he was looking forward to eating something nice.

The truth was, David's dad was shy. When he was testing people's eyes, they would sometimes try to chat with him, but he never knew what to say. He'd just grunt and quickly get on with his work. Or he'd try to smile and answer them, but it came out all wrong and everyone would be embarrassed for him and wish they'd never said anything at all.

It took Terry ages to get to know people, but once he did make friends he really loved them and if they went away, it broke his heart. It broke his heart when his wife left him. And it broke his heart all over again every time David told him he wanted to live with his mum—which he did about six times a week to start with. He felt that David was the only thing in his life worth having, but he wasn't very good at showing how much he loved him and all he ever seemed to do was worry and shout, worry and shout. David had got used to the fact that he wasn't ever going to live with his mum again, but ever since she'd left, he'd been getting into worse and worse trouble at school.

When Terry came back from work that day, there was more trouble. David's clothes were covered in filthy, greasy dust. "What happened to you?" his dad demanded.

"I don't know," lied David. He'd cleaned his hands and face and the sofa, but he hadn't even noticed his clothes. In the end he had to pretend that he'd crawled into a trash can, because his dad insisted on an explanation. He was amazed that his dad believed him. He had to do the dishes after dinner as a punishment.

2

Exploring the Ducts

David began to dream about having a secret life in the ducts.

The people he could spy on! He could listen to what they said when they thought no one could hear them, watch what they did when they thought they were alone. He could discover his neighbors' secrets. He could catch thieves, forgers, and murderers. He could be a hero. Who knew how many of his neighbors in Mahogany Villas were really criminals, pretending to live ordinary lives but actually forging twenty-pound notes or hoarding kidnapped children and stolen jewelry in their living rooms?

Or he could come out of the vents and steal whatever he wanted and they wouldn't be able to do a thing about it.

"Ah can't unnerstan' where it's goin' to!" said David. He was imitating Mr. Hadrian, who lived two floors below and was always moaning about the cost of living.

Oh, you could be wicked, all right, if you had a secret life behind the walls. He thought about telling his friends about the ducts—but not yet. This was his secret. He wasn't ready to share it. And there was another reason for keeping quiet. The vents were a tight fit; he doubted if any of his friends were small enough to squeeze in. He'd just get teased for being small again. Pavement Wiper, Short Ass, Bum Wipe! He hated all that.

These were wonderful thoughts, but somehow, in the back of his mind, David was sure it wasn't going to happen. It was dreams. Dreams are no good if you admit that they aren't likely to come true, but it was a bit like winning the lottery. It happened in newspapers and it happened in movies and books, but it never happened to you. Catching criminals? Spying, stealing in from the ducts, and carrying valuables away? Well, of course he'd do it, he'd do it all . . . sometime.

So one week went by, and then another. David

13

began to forget all about the ducts. He might never have gone in there again, but then he got grounded for a week.

He and Tyne Williams had set off together after school. They didn't hang around much together, but all the other kids had gone home and they didn't have anywhere to go since they didn't have parents at home—it was a Thursday, another of the days when Terry worked late. So they set off. They wandered across London as far as Kings Cross and hung about the tube, trying to spot prostitutes and drug dealers.

"Let's cross the river," said Tyne.

"Nah," said David. "Too far."

"Let's go to Kilburn."

"Yeah, okay."

So then they went to Kilburn. On the way back, after spending all that time together, Tyne suddenly started on David, nagging away about how short he was. He invented a new name, Clockwork, because David's little leggies had to go so fast to keep up with everyone else. On and on he went. "All right, Clockwork? D'you want me to slow down, Clockwork? I'm going to tell everyone at school your new name."

There was a fight in which David backed Tyne up to a skip and then ducked down, grabbed his knees, and upended him backward into the rubbish. There was glass at the bottom of the skip and Tyne cut his shoulder badly. It needed stitches. David ran home, leaving Tyne wailing and shrieking from inside the skip. They were both scared stiff because of the blood.

"Kings Cross," seethed his dad. It was a very seedy area, which is why they'd gone. "Kilburn! Miles away! Fighting in the street, in the rubbish. Of course he got cut, of course skips are full of all sorts of sharp rubbish."

"I didn't know about the glass," said David, not at all sorry. And so he got grounded for a week. That meant two hours after school each day before his dad got back and five hours on Tuesday and Thursday, with nothing to do.

David could have skived off the grounding most of the time since his dad wouldn't be there, but he was sick of the kids at school. Tyne had told everyone about the new name, and it was Clockwork this and Clockwork that. The nice kids didn't call him names, but although he liked some of the nice kids, he didn't want to hang around with them. He wanted to hang around with the bad kids. So he got into a couple of fights, made sure he didn't get caught, and went home straightaway without playing with anyone.

At home he watched TV on the first night, but already he was thinking about the world behind the walls. He knew he was going back in there sometime over the next week. Once he'd made up his mind, it happened quickly.

The next day he came home, ate a chocolate biscuit, drank some milk, and then straightaway pushed the sofa up against the wall. Before he climbed up, he went to change his clothes, so he wouldn't have to explain about the dirt again. He took some fresh batteries for the flashlight out of the drawer and a pencil and paper to make a map of his travels. He went to the storage cupboard and brought out a piece of thick board that his dad had left over from making shelves. He knew what he was up to. He could think ahead if he wanted to. He'd been planning it all day.

Now he was ready. He got up on the back of the sofa, pushed the grille to one side, and put his head in.

He'd forgotten how dark it was. Deep dark, creepy dark. Once again he had a feeling that the darkness was haunted. It was as if the dark was alive.

Yet not for a moment did he consider not going in. That was David for you. Just because he was scared out of his wits, he had to do it.

He turned on the flashlight and the darkness disappeared.

"Right," he muttered.

He picked up the piece of board from the sofa beside him, pushed it into the duct in front of him, and pulled himself up after it. Once his knees were up, he worked quickly, shoving it forward until the board lay over the big duct that led like the throat of the building, down to who knows where.

He'd brought the board in to cover the pit so that he wouldn't fall down it. Also, if there *was* anything down there, maybe the board would keep it trapped. He didn't think a piece of board would really stop anything from coming up, but then, he didn't really believe in ghosts, either. But it felt better, anyway.

David sat for a while on the bridge he'd made, just doing nothing. It was thrilling. Underneath him was a bottomless pit with a living darkness in it, but it couldn't get to him. He'd defeated the ghost—not that he believed in it—with his piece of thick board. After a while he got fed up just sitting there and decided to go exploring. He drew an arrow on the board to show the way home, even though he could see the light just behind him. Then he turned left and crawled off to explore the ducts.

That was scary, because it meant turning away out of sight of the apartment. There was a terrifying, sweaty crawl with his heart banging away inside him. He kept stopping to look back in case something was creeping up behind him. He hated not behind able to turn around. But it was worth it. He soon came to another offshoot from the main duct. He peered down it, and at the end there was another grille.

He'd found the way to his next-door neighbor, Mary Turner. She was a teacher, but she wouldn't be back from work yet. He'd never been inside her apartment. He crawled quietly to the grille and peered in.

He could see everything. A tank of goldfish turned all green. A sofa strewn with clothes, including various pieces of underwear. There were wrappers to candy bars and a greasy bucket of Kentucky Fried Chicken, with the chips spilled onto the floor. There was a puddle of tea or coffee or something on the coffee table that had dripped down onto the badly stained red-and-yellow carpet. Mary always dressed in neat clothes and looked prim and proper. But she wasn't. Her place was a complete pigsty.

David was thrilled. Her apartment wasn't anything like you'd think. Who knows what she got up to on her own—and he'd be able to watch her at it.

The grille was just the same as the one in his apartment. He could move it aside easily enough with his fingers, but he wasn't sure when she was coming home, so he didn't go inside. Not this time. Instead, he crawled back the way he'd come. There was a nasty moment when he had to push his legs out unseen into the main duct—he could just imagine something horrible sitting in the darkness watching him. But of course there was nothing there, just his own fear.

Looking farther along the duct, David could see other patches of light coming in from other ducts leading to other apartments. He thought—Just one more. Next door but one lived Alan and Jo Winsome with their little boy, George. That would be interesting.

David crawled along to their duct and peeped down to where it ended in another grille. The light was on. He could hear the television muttering away—children's TV. They must be in. He just had to have a peek.

He went as quietly as he could, but it was impossible not to make some noise. He got around the corner into the duct that led to their apartment quietly enough, but as soon as he tried to crawl forward his knees rattled on the metal. David paused, frozen, waiting to be discovered. But it was the voice of a small child who called out,

"Who is it?"

David stayed very still. After a long wait in which nothing happened, he began to edge away, but as he did, he made more noise. Poor George—he was only four—called out again tearfully, "I'll tell my mum when she comes home."

So—Georgie was on his own. David stopped crawling and waited a while, listening. He wasn't scared of any little kid who hadn't even started school yet. He took a deep breath and he went, "Ooooooooo ooooooo oooooo . . . ," in a long ghostly voice. In the apartment George whimpered. Sniggering to himself, David crawled farther backward until he got to Mary's offshoot. He sat there for a bit, feeling guilty. Poor kid! A voice coming out of the wall! So he crawled forward again, made a bit of noise, listened, and then said in a more gentle voice, "It's all right, George, it's allriiiiiiight." Then he scurried backward again, snorting with laughter. He knew what he was doing. Having a ghost behind the wall telling you it was all right was definitely *not* all right.

He crawled back until he came to the shelf over the big duct and he sat on that a bit more. It was a good place. He could see right into his own apartment, and he could sit or even stand upright because the big duct carried on up overhead. It felt private. It felt great. It felt safe.

Haunted indeed! He'd been right inside and there was nothing. He began drawing a little map of where he'd been, but he could remember it all so clearly, he didn't bother. Instead, he sat there daydreaming again about all the things he could see and do in these secret ways.

Next time, he'd go farther. Next time, he'd go right into someone's apartment—Mary's probably. Who'd have thought what a dirty old bag she was. Maybe he'd tidy her apartment up. That would give her a shock!

3

Mr. Alveston

It was just great. On the very first time he'd ghosted out a little kid and seen Mary Turner's underwear lying around on her sofa. You bet that little kid believed in ghosts now! Mary was a teacher at a high school. If David had gone to that high school, he'd have said to the kids in her class, "Do, you want to know what color underpants she wears?" And he'd be able to tell them. If he got there early enough in the morning, he might even be able to watch her put them on.

David spent the next couple of days at school

daydreaming about the fun still to come. He was going to watch people walking around half dressed, men shaving and singing to themselves out of tune, like idiots. Picking their noses, probably. People talking to themselves. It was great; he'd be like a hidden camera. He could take photos and blackmail people. He could watch women with nothing on. He could see Mary Turner with nothing on. He knew she had a boyfriend. Maybe he'd be able to spy on them together.

All thoughts of catching thieves and being a hero had gone by this time. Being good just wasn't practical, he realized. As soon as he came out of the ducts to do his good deed, he'd give the game away. If he saw a strange man robbing an apartment, he'd just have to watch. If he went and told, the police would ask him, "What were you doing in there, anyway?" Then they'd find out how he'd been spying on people. No—good deeds were out.

Anyway, there was something about the ducts that made David feel bad. He didn't know what it was, but every time he thought about it, he felt bad, thought bad, and wanted to do bad. In fact, David was looking forward to behaving worse than he ever had in his whole life. It was just great. He couldn't wait to get back in and have another go.

• • •

As David was walking home from school that Thursday, thinking about things to come, an old, old man who lived on the floor above him was day-dreaming about things that had already happened. The old man was called Robert Alveston. He'd been born in London in the year 1904 and he remembered so much that it was hard for him to concentrate on what was going on right now.

Mr. Alveston had grown up in London, but he'd lived all over the world. The last time he'd lived in London, when he was sixty-four, he'd fallen in love with a handsome, plump florist, whose name was Rose. They got married within a month. She was his second wife and he loved her more than anyone. He called her Tulip for fun.

They ran a florist's shop in Chiswick for ten years. Then, in their midseventies, they decided to go and live in France before they were too old to do it. They went to Paris and enjoyed a happy marriage of over twenty years before Tulip died of a stroke at the age of eighty-two. Mr. Alveston didn't want to stay in the house they'd shared together. London was where he'd been born, where he'd met his beloved Tulip, and that's where he decided to end his days.

So he came back, but he soon found out that he'd

24

made a bad mistake. Most of the people he and Tulip used to know had moved on, died, or else become so old themselves that they barely ever got out.

So it was that despite having lived a life filled with people, he'd somehow ended up with no one. His children, a boy and a girl, had already died of old age. His grandchildren and great-grandchildren lived in Australia. He had friends all around the world. Someone wrote or telephoned him every day, but that wasn't the real thing. He used to sit for hours in his armchair, wondering what on earth had happened. How was it that you could be sur-rounded by people for more than ninety years and then suddenly have no one at all to drop by on for a cup of tea and a chat?

To make matters worse, he was going a bit crazy. He knew he was going a bit crazy because the neighbors worried about him and the social worker kept stopping in to check on him and offering to put him into a home. He kept forgetting what he was doing. For instance, there was the day he'd spent all morning wandering about his apartment looking for his false teeth when they were actually in his mouth the whole time. There were other times when he forgot what road or even what town or country he lived in, and he'd get all panicky about finding himself in a strange apartment, even if it did have all his own things in it.

When this happened, he told himself that he was having a "senior moment" and laughed at himself. But there was no one to share the joke, so what was the point?

There were the neighbors, they were very kind, but they all seemed to have full lives without room to make a new friendship with the likes of him. Even so, Mr. Alveston made the best of it. He joined a bridge club; he went out every day to do his shopping and chatted with the shopkeepers. He called on his neighbors and they called on him. But one thing above all kept him going—the brilliant, crystal-clear memories of his past lives, of which there were so many.

He could remember everything. His childhood. His two elder brothers, both of whom had died in the Great War; his sister, Susan, who had lost her sweetheart at the same time. She'd cried for a month. His first wife, Greta, whom he had married in 1926. They lived in Germany together. They had huge window boxes full of geraniums that needed to be watered three times a day in summer. Greta used to boast about it. Each winter they used to go skiing in the Alps. She was miles better than him.

She used to shoot past him and spray him with snow. He could still hear her giggle as she sped off downhill and he could remember every snowflake that flew up from under her skis.

On weekends in the summer they often went swimming in great, cool, wooded lakes with their two children, Alex and Nadja. Mr. Alveston remembered every day at every lake, whether the water was soft and cloudy and warm, or crystal clear and icy cold. He could remember every hair on his children's heads from the ages of zero to twenty, when they finally left home. He could remember the day Greta died in a car accident, how the police came to the door, and how he'd wept for the first time in front of his children. A few months later he'd gone to live in Australia with the children, to get away from the war in Europe.

He spent all morning one day reliving the time he'd been a smuggler and taken a hundred gallons of brandy in a small boat over the sea from France into England with his friend Alain. They'd been chased and caught by the customs boat and had to pour the brandy overboard. While the customs men were questioning them, a dolphin started banging into the boat and Alain swore it was drunk.

And of course there were the times with the

wonderful, wonderful Tulip. They used to go to the flower market together to buy roses, lilies, chrysanthemums, and other flowers. They dowsed them in water, drove back to the shop with them, and arranged them in huge, splendid bunches on the pavement outside their shop. He could remember those days second by second, and the petals in every flower. How he had loved the flowers! How he had loved Tulip!

Robert's memories were so clear that they took over his life. As he walked along the streets he talked to people long dead. As he sat in his chair he believed he was ten again, or seventeen, or fifty or sixty or only three years old.

On this very day, this same day when David was walking back from school with an evil thought in his hot head, Robert Alveston sat down in his armchair under the ventilation grille on the wall and remembered. His memories were solid things; he could hear them, smell them, taste them. He was at that very moment remembering when he used to play with his friends on the streets of London, when he was a child, back in the days when you could wander for miles, and the roads were heaving with horses and you hardly ever saw an automobile, and the whole world was there for your fun, so long as you never got caught. . . .

. . .

David banged open the rattling grille door on the old elevator in Mahogany Villas and ran down the gloomy hall to his apartment. His father was working late and David had hours of spying and wickedness ahead of him.

He wasted no time at all changing his clothes, getting the sofa over by the wall, and then taking off the grille. Once again, that eye of darkness in the wall was staring at him, and once again, he stood on the back of the sofa and shivered. Why did he forget every time what it was like in there? So dark, so *narrow*. Just looking in, he felt as if the darkness could squeeze him to death.

But David wasn't going to be put off by things he couldn't even see. He turned on his flashlight, pulled himself up, and wriggled inside the walls of Mahogany Villas.

The first thing he did was crawl along to have a look in Mary's apartment. Once again the crawl was dirty and frightening, and when he finally got there—what a disappointment! She'd cleaned up. Everything was neat and tidy; the only personal thing he could see was a towel hanging over the back of a chair. He thought about taking the grille out and going in, but he didn't dare. Not yet. Sometimes Mary came home early.

He crawled down to Alan and Jo and Georgie's place. He could hear voices. Jo Winsome was there with a friend. Their voices boomed and echoed in the narrow ducts. It was no good at all. David knew at once he could never get any closer to the grille without attracting attention. Even so far away, they could hear him. As he was creeping quietly off he was sure he heard Jo ask, "What was that noise?" and he had to lie as still as he could for minutes on end before they left the room and he was able to make his escape.

David was furious. He crawled back to his place on the board over the duct and cursed silently. Why was nothing ever as good as it should be? He clenched his fists and hissed in frustration. He didn't dare make a noise, but all he wanted to do was roll over onto his back and kick until the whole place rang out. Mahogany Villas would be filled with noise and nobody would know where it came from. Kids would have nightmares! The apartment building would be haunted; everyone would believe in ghosts then! But he didn't dare for fear of being caught.

That was when he stood up. You could do that in the big duct. Under him were the dark places below. Around him were the close sides of the duct. Above him was the next floor. If he shone his flashlight up, he could see where the duct opened up into another duct going across. That would lead to all the apartments on the fifth floor. Maybe he'd have better luck up there.

David looked at his watch. He had two hours still to go. He bent his knees and arched his back and wedged himself tightly into the big duct. He could climb up, no problem! He lifted his hands and began to climb.

It was hard going, but it wasn't far. The way up wasn't as dirty as the way along. He had a good grip and didn't slip once. The worst thing was the dark. He needed both hands to climb with and had to tuck the flashlight, still on, down his jeans. Flickering shadows writhed and twisted up the duct like phantoms, but he didn't dare turn it off.

He pushed and shoved as fast as he could, and at last he was able to get his hands into the duct running along the next floor and heave himself up. He hung with his arms over the edge, pulled the flashlight out, and shone it along the new duct.

It was just the same as the one below had been before he crawled along it. It was covered with an even, smooth layer of greasy dust. It reminded David of a fresh fall of new snow.

David pulled himself along the duct. He didn't like being so far from home, but he wouldn't give in.

Under him the new dust turned black against his chest and legs. Another few feet and he was at the first offshoot to an apartment on the fifth floor. David looked down the duct to the apartment and saw that at the end of it, the grille was missing.

He ducked back quickly out of sight. The grilles were like locked gates. Why was this one off?

After a little while, when there was no noise, he poked his head cautiously around to have another look.

Inside the apartment it was dull. Maybe it was being decorated. He remembered how his dad had taken the grille off once when he was decorating. He waited a long time but heard nothing—no voices, no radio or television—so he plucked up his courage and slid like a snake down toward the opening to try and see inside.

He tried to be quiet, but some scufflings had to happen. At one point he forgot himself and banged hard on the metal. He froze—but there was still no noise. It must be that no one was in. He got to the lip of the duct, waited just to be sure there was no noise, then pulled himself forward on his stomach and peered in.

Right down below him was an old man sitting in an armchair. As David stared, the old man opened his eyes and looked up. David yelped. For one horrible moment they stared straight into each other's faces, and then the old man opened his mouth and said,

"Jonathon!"

David couldn't turn, so he pushed himself back, shoving with his hands, scooting backward the way he'd come. He went as fast as he could, but he didn't go fast enough. In front of David, framed by the end of the duct, there now appeared a floating face, but not the man's face. It was the gray face of a boy. The boy's mouth was open, he was yelling, but there was no sound. Then, right through that face, another face appeared—that of the old man. He must have got a chair to stand on. David yelped with terror. He could see *through* the boy! He buried his own face in his arms so he couldn't be recognized and pushed with his elbows to scoot himself the final few feet back into the main duct.

"Come back!" pleaded the old man. But David was going fast. He scuttled backward to the junction as the old man waved and grinned and begged him not to go. David popped out into the big duct, turned around, and shot like a ferret toward the duct. He was clanging and banging away like a spanner in the works. He got to the way down and paused, hanging over it, holding himself up on his hands and legs like a spider, ready to drop. But before he went, he had to look back, he just had to, so he stopped, ducked his head, and peered back from between his legs.

The ghost was rushing forward toward David. As he came he grew bigger and bigger, until he was like a truck charging through the ducts. David screamed and the ghostly boy opened his mouth and screamed back. But his scream wasn't the scream of a child. It was the scream of an old, old man. "Come back, come back," screamed the ghost in his cracked old voice. "Don't leave me. Don't go!"

David let go and fell like a stone three feet down to the board below. He lay panting for seconds, listening to the old man's desperate calls. He twisted and looked up just in time to see the pale frightened face of the ghostly boy looking down at him. The mouth opened.

"Don't leave me," came the voice of the old man from far away. David screamed again, "Go away!" Then he pushed himself out of the duct and plopped into the safety of his own home.

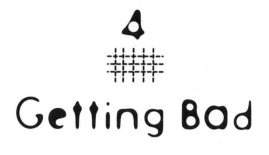

Getting Bad

As soon as David tumbled out onto the carpet he jumped back up and began tidying up before his dad came home. He wiped the dirt marks off the floor and the wall where he'd fallen out; he put the grille back on. All the time he could feel his legs shaking underneath him and a thin fizz of pure terror tingling in every vein.

Ghosts! He'd never really believed in them, but now he'd seen one. The grille in the wall led from home to the secret haunting place. There were secrets in the wandering metal tubes that ran all around Mahogany Villas.

"What's up with you tonight?" his dad kept asking him, but David just shook his head. Terry wondered if he was being picked on at school again for being small, and he bit his lip. He hated to think of his son being bullied, but since David would never admit to it unless he got caught fighting, there was nothing anyone could do about it.

David went to bed that night shivering with fear. And yet . . . The strange thing was, after seeing what he'd seen and hearing what he'd heard, he was already beginning to disbelieve it all. He'd been scared. He'd panicked, that was all. He'd just imagined that there was something there. The pale face and the slight figure hurrying and banging and growing so huge, even though there was no room for it to get huge . . . that long face staring down at him with its mouth wide open as if it was shouting, but the old man's voice coming from far away . . . It was impossible! It was just his imagination, surely?

The ducts opened up into every room in the apartment and that night David lay in his bed and stared at the square darkness of the grille on his bedroom wall. What was in there? Could it come out to find him in the night?

"You big baby!" he told himself. But the mere thought of going into the ducts at night made his whole skin sparkle with fear.

Oh, David was scared; he was scared silly. But being David, being scared just made him want to do more.

"Is there anyone in there?" he called softly. From the ducts, there was no reply. All he had to do to prove it was creep across the room and look in.

At night? In the dark?

Of course, it was always nighttime in the ducts, but that didn't stop the night dark from being worse than the day dark. Even so, a moment later David got out of bed, took his chair over to the wall, and stood up on it so that his head was just on a level with the grille. He could feel the cool air moving from inside on his cheek.

David held his breath and listened. From far, far away, he could hear the soft sound of someone crying. A boy. It didn't sound at all dangerous; it sounded sad, so very sad. He stood there for a whole minute, listening to the noise, trying to convince himself that it was some child in one of the other apartments who was weeping. Georgie, perhaps.

"Who's there?" he called softly. At once, the crying stopped. A thrill of horror ran through him. If it was a child in a room, surely he wouldn't have heard him. Whoever—whatever—was doing the weeping, it had to be in the ducts.

"It's all right, don't cry," said David. There was no more sound. A second later he lost his nerve and ran back to bed.

The next day at school it was as if none of it had happened. Weeping ghosts, boys screaming in old men's voices—that wasn't real life. Catching the bus, doing lessons, fighting back at the kids who were calling him Clockwork—that was real life. The ducts were like that. They took him over when he was inside, but in the daylight it all seemed impossible, far away, like a dream or a movie you'd watched in the multiplex weeks ago.

On the way home David stopped in the entrance to Mahogany Villas and read down the long lists of names by the doorbells. Fifth floor. He counted along. The old man had been in the apartment above his, next one along. He couldn't quite work out which bell was which, though, and he had to ride up on the elevator to find the number and then look it up.

Number 501. Mr. Robert Alveston.

"Do you know Mr. Alveston?" he asked his dad while they were eating dinner.

"The old man on the floor above ours?" asked his dad.

"Yes."

"What do you know about him?" his dad wanted to know, but David was ready with a lie.

"He just started talking to me in the lobby yesterday," he said with a little shrug, as if it didn't matter at all.

"They're always talking about him during residents' meetings," said his dad. "Asking people to keep an eye on him and visit him and things. He's gone a bit crazy. A touch of Alzheimer's."

"What?"

"A bit senile. The social services are keeping an eye on him. He gets lost, can't find his way back to his apartment. Talks to people when there's no one there, that sort of thing. His eyesight's not so good; his hearing's on the blink. Falling to bits, really, but he's as sharp as anything on a good day. He ought to be in a home but hates the idea, poor old guy."

"What about his family—why don't they look after him?"

"Well, he says there's grandchildren somewhere, but no one's ever seen them."

"Has he got a son?" asked David, wondering who Jonathon was. But Terry couldn't remember.

That night David stuck a poster over the grille even though he knew a poster couldn't stop anything. He drew a cross with a felt tip pen on the poster and rubbed it with garlic to keep off vampires. He thought about going to the church to steal some holy water, but then he thought stolen holy water probably wouldn't work.

The next Thursday, he went wandering off with Tyne again, and this time they stayed friends. Tyne showed him an old run-down house that they went into and explored together. It was great. They bought some doughnuts and Tyne apologized for calling him Clockwork.

He got back after his dad and got into more trouble for being late. He didn't care. When his dad heard that he'd made friends with Tyne, he forgave him. David thought about telling his dad about the ghost, but decided it was impossible. Terry didn't believe in ghosts either. All he'd want to know about was why David had been sneaking about inside the building and spying on people.

The days ticked by. Then it was Tuesday; his dad was working late again. David had almost stopped thinking about the ducts, but to his own horror, as soon as he was at home on his own with a few hours to spare, he went straight back inside. It was amazing how quickly it happened. He just came back from school, got changed, and, without even thinking about it, pushed the sofa to the wall and climbed in. It was like he had no choice in the matter. He was sitting on the board, looking up along his flash-light beam with his heart hammering away inside him, before it even occurred to him that he didn't have to go in if he didn't want to.

He did Mary Turner's apartment first. It was a mess again. She'd been eating chips and drinking beer, and it looked as though she'd had a chip fight with someone. There were beer cans and crushed chips everywhere.

"What on earth does she get up to?" David wondered.

He slid the grille off and climbed down into the apartment.

Inside, he wandered about, poking inside drawers and cupboards, looking for anything private. He drank some juice out of her fridge and finished off a bag of half-eaten chips that was lying on the floor. There was a pair of long brown boots, one on each side of the settee, with long rows of eyes for the laces up the sides. David took the left one back into the duct when he left. He thought that was hilarious. He kept giggling at the thought of Mary Turner wandering about for hours, searching for her lost boot. She'd never find it! He was still laughing when he reached the big upright duct outside his apart-ment, but when he heard an answering giggle com-ing down from over his head, he shut up.

An echo? Or a ghost . . .

He shone his beam up there. Nothing. The laugh must have been an echo. After waiting a long, long time in the silence, David climbed up to the fifth floor. Here he sat on the edge of the big duct for another long time, waiting for the slightest hint of movement or noise, but there was nothing, except of course for the oddness of being in there in the first place. On the dust he could see the marks he had made crawling backward and forward before. The laugh he had heard must have been an echo. There were all sorts of odd noises and echoes in a place like this, coming in from the various apartments through the grilles and creeping like spooks around the ducts.

David began to creep along the ducts. When he got to the offshoot that led to Mr. Alveston's apartment, he lay out of sight just around the corner, listening.

Voices. It might be the TV, but he couldn't be sure. He peeped around the corner. The grille was still off, but he couldn't see anything. Then there was a click. It was the TV being turned off. But one of the voices carried on. It was the old man. He'd been talking to the people on the TV—the silly old fool!

David listened as hard as he could, but he couldn't make out what the old man was saying to himself. He wanted to go closer, but he didn't dare in case he got seen. It would take the old man just a moment to get up on the chair, and he'd be stuck like a rat in a trap.

It was very frustrating. Quite suddenly, fed up with not being able to do what he wanted to do, David decided he'd had enough of this game. Just as it looked as if there was something really good about it, it turned out you couldn't do it after all. What was the point? What was the point of the old man being blind, deaf, and daft if you couldn't do anything? David decided that he'd never bother coming back into the ducts again. This was going to be his last trip—and at the same time, that meant he could do absolutely anything he wanted. Without even thinking any more about it, he put his hands to his mouth and said in a low, hooting voice,

"Heeellooo, Mr. Robert Aaaaaalveston. This is Jonathon, Jonathon speeeeakiiiing. Ooooooo, ooooo . . ."

At once the muttering voice stopped. David started sniggering desperately. It was so funny—*he* was the ghost behind the walls! He put his hands over his mouth and spluttered.

"Who's there?" called the old voice anxiously.

"Ohhhh, Mr. Alveston, ohhh, beware, bewaaaaare, I am the ghost of Jonathon, whooooo!" David burst out chortling. It was so gloriously bad! He didn't even try covering up his laughter. The old man would never know who was playing this trick on him. He must be scared silly! For the first time David wished he had someone with him to share this great joke with.

"Whooo, Jonathon, ooooooo. I am Jonathon," boomed David in a loud voice, and he cracked up laughing to himself.

And then from the duct in front of him came another voice floating down.

"Jonathon . . . Jonathon, woooo, oooo, woooo, beware, Jonathon . . ."

That was no echo! David looked up—and there was the ghost. He was in the ducts two or three apartments ahead, lying on his stomach in exactly the same position as David. He was copying him. He had his hands to his mouth in the same way and he was saying the same thing. He was killing himself laughing.

David yelled out in fright. He jumped up and banged his head, and the other boy started laughing at that, too. What made David feel sick was the way he could see straight through him. It made him shudder all over. Then the boy began crawling forward toward David. He was using his hands, one in front of the other, but he was sliding forward as if he was on rollers, as if he was only pretending that he moved in the same way as a person did.

"Go away! Just stay away! Leave me alone!" It was the old man shouting. The boy pulled a strange face—David didn't know if he was laughing or crying—and then he howled, "Wooo, beware. You silly old fooooool!" he wailed.

David shouted, "Stay away! Stay away!" and began to crawl backward. But the boy kept on crawling toward him faster than ever. His face seemed to be going faster than the rest of him. It was reaching beyond his body and coming toward David as if it was on a stick in the most horrible manner, still half grinning, half crying, and wailing, "Silly old fooooooooool!"

"No!" screamed David in terror, but the boy came on. In another second David could feel the edge of the duct on his ankles. With one last desperate push backward, he hurled himself down.

"No! Please!" wailed the boy.

"Go away!" bellowed the old man. Without waiting another second, David shoved himself violently backward and popped out of the hole in the wall into his apartment. He came out so fast that he missed the sofa altogether and fell heavily on his shoulder onto the floor.

"Don't go! Play with me!" screeched the boy.

"Leave me alone!" wailed the old man. David was certain that both of them were coming after him. Jumping up, he fitted the grille back into place and then stood there, pressing it to the wall and staring at the darkness he had just imprisoned. Just for a second he saw something there—the pale, terrified face of the ghost boy staring back out at him. David snatched his hands away. Then the face disappeared so suddenly, it looked as if it had been snatched away or blown off in a gale. A slight sprinkle of dust fell from the bars of the grille.

For almost ten minutes David stayed glued to that grille, staring like a mad dog into the space behind the walls, too scared to move in case the ghost came back. Then he sighed deeply, put his hands to his face, and said, "Man, that was bad, that was really bad." He felt like crying, but he didn't have time. He had to clean up and get everything sorted out for when his dad came home.

Back in apartment 501, Robert Alveston was sitting in his armchair with his head in his hands, his heart beating fearfully in his chest.

It was getting worse!

It had started with him just forgetting where he put things—teaspoons and cups, his keys, his wallet. It was so frustrating; he always used to have a memory like a jewel. Next he'd started not recognizing things. It wasn't just faces or people. It was everyday things. The first time it happened in a big way, it had been with a teapot. He saw it on the stove and he just hadn't got a clue what it was. "Whatever is that *thing*? What on earth is it for?" he muttered to himself. He thought it looked hilarious, with its fat body and its funny, bendy, spouty thing sticking out. He had to keep going into the kitchen to have another look at it and laugh. "What a stupid-looking thing!" he said with a giggle. Hilarious! Then he forgot that he didn't know what it was for and made himself a cup of tea, and it wasn't until the next day that he suddenly remembered that he'd forgotten what it was for three whole hours.

In one way it was quite funny. He'd enjoyed not knowing what a teapot was; it had been good fun. You saw things so freshly. But it was a very worrying thing nonetheless.

The next thing was, he'd started finding himself with no memory at all of what he had been doing for the past hours or minutes. The other day he had found himself with a pair of scissors in his hands, busy cutting his trousers in half. He had a vague, fleeting memory that someone had hidden treasure in the pockets—but what for, or why that meant he had to cut them in half, he had no idea.

It was as if his dreams had taken over his life. It made him scared he'd have a nightmare. And now look! He'd started to imagine things.

The first time it had happened, he was sitting quietly in his room, daydreaming about something that had happened to him as a child.

It was early summer. He was a boy, eleven years old. He could smell the hot roads and the horses that pulled the coaches and carriages up and down the streets, and the stink of the occasional automobile that went chugging past. He was out with a friend of his, a boy called Jonathon Price. They were sneaking into some farm plots in Kentish Town, hoping to steal some new carrots or find pods of green peas. They'd walked along the tall rows of beans, watched the potato flowers bobble about under the weight of the bees and hoverflies.

For Mr. Alveston this wasn't just a memory; he was *there*. He could smell the earth. He could hear the bees buzzing in the flowers. If he'd touched one, it would have stung him. At his side, his friend Jonathon walked along, pulling baby beans off the plants and eating them.

They turned a corner and ran into a man weeding with a hoe. Jonathon thought they'd been caught and ran off, but Robert knew the man: it was Mr. Jonston, a neighbor of his. He had quite a job convincing Jonathon to stay. Mr. Jonston let them pull a couple of carrots out of the ground and wiped the dirt off for them, and then he invited them to help him dig up the early potatoes. That was good! They levered the trowels up in the black earth, and there were the spuds hidden in the ground, spilling out like cool, earthy treasure. Robert speared one on the trowel, and the neighbor said, "Try and dig a bit farther away from the plant; that one's no good now."

Robert looked up at the man and smiled . . . and at that very moment he heard the rattle in the ventilation shaft over his head. He looked up, an old man dozing in his chair once more, and saw the boy ducking out of sight. At the same time, on the ground at his feet, there was another boy. It was a boy he knew, he was sure he knew him; he knew him as well as he knew himself, but at that moment he had no idea who exactly it was. The boy looked at him, and in a single bound, like something in a movie, like a cat or some kind of imp, he had leapt up into the ventilation shaft and was gone.

Hurriedly Mr. Alveston pulled a chair over to the wall, climbed up, and peered in, just in time to see the first boy backing off around the corner in the ductwork. The switch from the past, which was so vivid, to the present, which was so strange, happened so quickly that he wasn't able to work out what was then and what was now. That was why he called out, "Jonathon!" after the boy; he thought for a moment that it was his friend going down the shaft.

The first boy turned the corner and went crashing off. As the old man watched, the second boy came back into view. There was a glimpse of a bony young face glaring down the duct at him. Then the boy was off, chasing after the other one as fast as he could.

"Come back—don't go!" cried the old man, certain that he knew this second boy from somewhere, if only he could remember where. But the boy was gone. All he could do was stand there and call uselessly after them.

It was crazy! The more he thought about it, the more certain he was that he had imagined the whole thing. Boys in the ventilation system? What next? Ladies in the sink, babies in the piano? Truly he was going mad. He'd get taken out of his own apartment and put in a home, which terrified him—

the social worker, Mrs. Grey, had been hinting at it for ages. Then he'd fall to bits and die surrounded by helpless old people, and he'd be wetting his bed and not knowing who he was or what was going on around him in no time.

And now it had happened again. He was hearing the same two boys jeering and hooting at him from behind the walls. What on earth was going wrong with him?

Mrs. Grey was due to visit later that day, but one thing he was certain of—he wasn't going to mention that voice teasing him from the ducts. They'd lock him away for sure if he said anything about that.

First his body had grown weak and slow, and now his mind was going as well. He felt like a small boy, lost in an immense dark place. He had no idea how he was going to get out of this trouble, or even if it was possible to escape. When your mind went, what did you have left? Not even yourself.

Sitting alone in his armchair, trying not to look at the fearful ventilator grille behind his head, Robert Alveston held his face and felt cold little tears run down between his fingers.

5

Mr. Alveston's Apartment

What are ghosts? The spirits of dead people, they say. Had a boy died in there long ago? Maybe he fell down one of the long ducts. Maybe there was a skeleton lying at the bottom, staring blindly up. Maybe it wanted David to make sure it got properly buried. Maybe it wanted him to join it.

That night David lay scaring himself silly with thoughts of monsters that could never die creeping in the dark behind the walls, waiting for him. But it hadn't been him the ghost was angry at. It was the old man it was after. Why? Was it just joining David in his nasty little games, or was there another reason for it haunting him?

Ghosts were supposed to come back from the dead to torment the people who had done them wrong in real life. Perhaps Mr. Alveston had done something terrible to the boy in the past. But what?

Was Mr. Alveston a murderer? How awful—to be living in the same apartment building as a murderer! If that was true, then the ghost only wanted its revenge. It wanted justice. Perhaps David ought to be feeling sorry for it, not scared of it, after all.

Once again, David left the warm safety of his bed and crept through the shadows to the grille in his wall. He listened for a long time with his ear close to the grille. He heard echoes and other dull noises that could have been anything. Only when he was about to give up did he hear a voice, very close to him.

"Play with me?" said the ghost, and with a little scream, David ran back to bed and hid his head under the covers. It was impossible! A voice must have traveled up the ducts from one of the apartments! He'd give anything not to have to believe that there was a real ghost there. For long hours David lay, with his head tucked just under the covers, straining to hear another whisper from the grille. But he heard no more. He fell asleep still shivering with fright and when he woke up, a sunbeam was shooting through a gap in his curtains. By the time he was out of bed and looking down at a bright sunny day outside, he was doubting that anything had happened at all. In the daylight such things seemed to be only nonsense, crazy dreams. But what dreams! And how well he remembered them!

"No, it wasn't a dream. It really happened," he said to himself. And all through the day the memories came back to him: the angry face of the boy, the terrified old man, the voice from the darkness begging him to come out to play . . .

A week passed. Two weeks. The adventure was beginning to fade. David was trying hard not to think about it at all and it was working quite well. If he never thought about it, it was the next-best thing to it never having happened. He'd put another poster up over the duct. He hadn't heard any noises for ages. It was all just going away. Then, one Monday after school, he met Mr. Alveston in the entrance of Mahogany Villas.

The old man was only little, just a head higher than David himself. He was so slight and frail, he looked as if you could break him in half by bumping into him. He had a cane in his hand and nodded politely as they passed in the lobby. He wore glasses and David could see the waxy splat of a hearing aid behind his ear. David nodded back. He was certain that the old man didn't know who he was.

"Good afternoon," he said politely.

"Hello, Tiger," said Mr. Alveston.

"What?" But the old man was smiling. He was joking.

"Grrrr," said David, and laughed. Mr. Alveston laughed, too.

"Nice to see someone with a bit of life in them," he said. He peered out up at the sky and saw gray, even cloud.

"Not raining, anyway," he said. He stepped carefully down off the step, as if he might slip and break a bit of himself off.

"Where are you going?" asked David. He wanted to know how long Mr. Alveston was going to be away.

It never occurred to the old man that David had anything bad in his head, and he smiled at the boy for his curiosity. "To the shops," he said. David noticed how he trembled—how his hand trembled on his cane, how his face and his whole body trembled. Not dangerous at all. Standing next to him in all his rough youth, David felt like he had once when he was in a shop selling china and glassware. He'd been scared to move in case he broke something.

Mr. Alveston smiled again at David, turned out of the lobby, and headed up the road. David went inside. The apartment would be empty for at least an hour. He ran upstairs, changed, and got into the ducts straightaway.

As usual, just before he went in, David stopped with his head inside and listened. His blood was banging in his ears. There was only the noise of the ducts—the noise of the darkness muttering and shuffling and turning over in its sleep. But there was something in the darkness. It was waiting for him and the funny thing was, David knew it was pleased to see him. It had missed him and it wanted him back.

"You and me. Let's do it!" it seemed to be saying. "Come on in—the darkness is lovely today!"

The ghost liked him!

David clambered in. He crawled to the duct going up and squirmed his way up to the floor above. Then he made his way on his belly like a snake directly toward Mr. Alveston's empty apartment. It only took a moment, then he was in the duct leading straight into the living room. The first thing he noticed was a sweet, thick scent filling the air. Then he was there, looking in.

Mr. Alveston's apartment was packed full of all sorts of things he'd gathered during his long life. There were little china figures, ornaments and vases and knickknacks covering the surfaces. The walls were covered with photos and paintings. There was a vase of white lilies with yellow stamens on a big table; it was their scent that filled the room. One whole wall was covered with books. On a little table near the window was a small, round box with a tiny model Santa Claus on the lid, with reindeer pulling a sled. Little elf figures were arranged in a circle around the edge. All around it was a crowd of tiny figures of angels playing musical instruments.

Robert and his wife Greta used to put these little figures out at Christmas to decorate the house for their two children.

David climbed down into the apartment.

The first thing he did was have a look at the fascinating little table with the Christmas things on it. The round box was a music box with a key still in it. When he wound it up, the top revolved, making the little Santa Claus and his elves go around in circles while the box played "Silent Night" in a clear, mellow tinkle.

David put the key to the music box in his pocket and turned his attention to the little figures. The angels were made of painted wood, all flaking with age. David rearranged them in a battle scene, some lying down as if they were dead, some head butting each other, some in a little heap to one side. One of them was playing a trombone made of golden wire, and he straightened the wire out and twisted it around another one's neck. He broke off a couple of arms and legs. He found a felt tip pen by the telephone and drew some ugly faces on the angels. Then he turned to have a look at the rest of the apartment and as he turned, he caught sight of the boy.

It was just a glimpse. He was standing next to the mantelpiece, grinning wildly and shouting something. But he had no voice. Then he turned and pointed to the mantelpiece and faded. It was like watching words vanish on a piece of paper. In just a few seconds he was gone.

David felt a prickle of excitement. A real ghost! Was it possible to be friends with a ghost?

David walked over to the mantelpiece to have a look. There were more of the little wooden angels playing instruments—it was the rest of the orchestra. David had already had his fun with the angels, but because he felt the boy wanted him to, he knocked more down and twisted their instruments and made another battlefield with them. And like a reward, the boy appeared again over by the little telephone table, bent double and howling with fun.

David was delighted. The horrible dangerous atmosphere of the dark ducts had all gone now. It was just fun. He had a friend—so what if he was a dead one? The things you could do with a ghost!

He looked around for more mischief. He turned some of the photos to face the wall and pulled handfuls of things out of the drawers. He went to the kitchen and drank some milk out of the bottle, then spat in it—and there was the ghost boy, over by the sink, clapping! He ate some chocolate biscuits out of a tin, trod one of them into the carpet, and hid the rest under the cushions in the living room. He used the toilet and peed on the floor. Then he spent some time rearranging things, moving the china from the mantelpiece to the windowsills, turning the doormat upside down. He scattered the sweet-scented lilies on the floor.

It was at that moment that one of the pictures fell off the wall. He was nowhere near it. It hit the ground and shattered. Then, as it lay on the floor, it broke again—just cracked into dozens of splinters as it lay flat on the ground with no one anywhere near it. He saw it quite clearly. It was exactly as if someone had stamped on it. But there was no foot.

"Be careful!" said David. He didn't want things getting out of hand. He went over to look at the picture. It was a photograph of Mr. Alveston, still old, but younger than he was now, standing arm in arm with a woman. This was his beloved Tulip, although of course David didn't know that.

"Don't break things," said David, but even as he spoke, another picture fell off the wall and crunched on the floor.

Ghosts weren't likely to do as you told them. David didn't want this—he was just having a bit of fun! He said, "What's your name?" just to try and change the subject, but there was no answer. Instead, everything went very still. Was the ghost offended? Had he said the wrong thing? Perhaps it had no idea who it was.

David decided that was enough. He walked back to the vent in the wall. "It's all right for you; I'm the one who'll get blamed," he said aloud. But there was no answer.

He climbed back into the ducts, listening anxiously for sounds of more breakages. It was a naughty ghost, that was for sure. It really enjoyed doing those bad things in the old man's apartment.

Just to show the ghost what else he could do, David went down into Mary Turner's apartment to fool around some more. He took her boot, which he had hidden in the ducts, back into her apartment and stole the other boot instead. That would confuse her! He also stole the remote to her TV, a bra she'd left on the back of a chair, and her hair dryer and took those to hide in the ducts. That was a big joke! He was partly showing off to the ghost, but it didn't show up. It only seemed to be interested in Mr. Alveston.

Back in the dark ducts, David glanced at his watch. It was almost six o'clock! Terror! His dad would be home at any time. He'd get caught!

He rushed back to try and get all the evidence out of the way before his dad came home.

As it happened, his dad was late that evening and to make up for it he bought fish-and-chips for dinner as a treat, but David was anything but grateful. In fact, he was furious and started scolding his dad for being late as soon as he stepped in the door. He kept on nagging all night. The truth of it was, he was scared silly by what he'd just done. It had been fun when he was there, but he had just been showing off. When he looked back on it, it was spooky and horrible.

As he ate his fish-and-chips he started having horrible fantasies about being found out. No one would believe his stories about a ghost. The police and social services would be called in. He'd be arrested. He might even be taken into foster care. He must have left fingerprints all over the place! Why didn't he think to wear gloves! Of course, he'd be blamed for what the ghost had done, too.

When his dad told him to help clear the plates away after dinner, he threw a huge fit. His dad infuriated him by calling it a tantrum, as if he was a baby, so he called him a big dummy and got sent to his room for an hour.

Later, when he sneaked out again after only fifteen minutes and his dad wanted to know why he was so touchy, he lied magnificently about being picked on at school. His dad was always worried about him being bullied because he was undersized. He was completely taken in. He said he'd call the school and have a word with them about it.

"Don't—I want to try to sort it out myself," David told him.

His dad smiled ruefully at his son's bravery. He was only a shorty himself and knew all about being teased.

"But you won't get into any fights?" he asked

anxiously. He knew that was David's usual way of solving problems.

"I don't think it'll come to that," said David. "Perhaps I'll have a word with the teachers myself."

Terry was so pleased with his son's grown-up attitude to the problem that he felt guilty as hell about sending him to his room and apologized to his son, as if it had been his own fault the whole time.

Robert Alveston had been having a good day. His memory, which came and went like a blackbird on the lawn, was firmly at home. He'd tidied the apartment up and written a letter to his grandchildren in Australia. He'd said nothing about the problems he'd been having lately. He didn't want to worry them. They had their own lives to live.

Every now and then one of them wrote inviting him to come and live with them, and he'd been seriously thinking about actually doing it. But now that he was going crazy, he was scared of turning to them. Who knew, pretty soon he might need round-the-clock care. His grandchildren had children of their own; they had busy lives. He'd just mess things up for them.

In the afternoon he went out to mail his letters and get some groceries. Lately he'd been getting the crazies, as he called them, at all sorts of inconvenient times, but this time everything was splendid. He got a herring and some new potatoes for his dinner. He was going to have the herring coated in oatmeal and fried in bacon fat. He got the ingredients for a cake, too. Jeremy Spalding, the chair of the residents' association, and the middle-aged lady with gray hair who lived with her husband a couple of doors down had both been popping in and out to see him lately, to lend him a hand and chat. He'd bake three cakes, one for each of them and one for himself, just to show he was still with it and knew how to show his gratitude.

He was looking forward to getting back home to his nice tidy apartment. He'd spent ages getting it perfect a couple of days ago. He'd done a good job and it had taken him this long to recover from the effort. The housework was getting beyond him. He was going to get a cleaning lady from the social services—there was one coming by to have a look tomorrow—and he wanted them to see that he still did his best. It was the first time in ages he'd got the place really clean. He had to admit it, the housework exhausted him.

But when he opened the door, nothing was as it should be. All his things had been switched around and messed up. Dreadful! He must have had another attack of the crazies before he left the house, but it had never been this bad before. The fridge door was wide open. He'd apparently eaten all the chocolate biscuits and left crumbs all over the carpet. He vividly remembered vacuuming, but he had no memory at all of eating the biscuits. The beautiful stargazer lilies he'd bought were all over the place, trodden on, broken. There was pee on the bathroom floor. It was horrible.

Worst of all, two of his favorite pictures of him and Tulip had been thrown to the floor and trampled on, and his display of Christmas ornaments from Germany was ruined. The little Engel Choir was scattered all over the table. The trombone had been straightened out and one of the angels was strangling another one with it. He'd drawn stupid, childish faces on the little things. The key to the music box was nowhere to be seen.

That music box was one of Robert's most precious possessions. His first thought was that perhaps he'd put the key in his pocket for safekeeping, although he never usually did that. He dropped his shopping on the floor and went all through his pockets. He put handfuls of change on the table, but the key wasn't there. Then he emptied the shopping on the sofa to see if he'd dropped it in there, but it wasn't there, either.

He began wandering around the apartment, muttering to himself and racking his brains, trying to remember what he'd done and where he'd left the key. It was dreadful! He'd started to go crazy even when he thought he was having a good day. There was no telling what he'd been up to. Perhaps he ought to go into a home after all, but the thought terrified him.

He began searching for the key, going through his pockets again in case he'd only *thought* he'd looked there but hadn't really. He looked again in the music box to see if he'd only imagined it wasn't there—once your mind started going, you couldn't trust anything, certainly not yourself. Then he went through all the cupboards and drawers, emptying things on the floor and scattering them about as he got more and more anxious. He even emptied the fridge. He even stuck his fingers in the butter to see if it was in there. He could have done *anything* without knowing about it! Look at the incident with the trousers. And that time he'd imagined he saw a child in the ventilation system.

Around and around the apartment he went, searching for the key that wasn't there, until everything was in complete chaos and he was utterly exhausted. He forgot all about the herring and his plans for cakes. He fed himself on a bag of currants and some walnuts he found on the floor and went to sleep without undressing, lying on a heap of clothes he'd emptied out of his drawers on top of the bed. He woke up in the middle of the night hot and sweaty and sticky, with his throat as dry as a piece of paper.

6

The Social Worker

Two middle-aged women were hurrying along, rattling their shoes in the halls of Mahogany Villas. They were on business.

"The worst thing is how distressed the poor old things get," said Alison Grey, the social worker. "Sometimes I think it's even worse at this stage, when they still know that something's gone wrong."

"I had an old gentleman who thought he was being haunted," said the other, an older woman called Sis Parkinson. "His name was Angel Fellman and he once sailed around the world in a tall ship. He was a deckhand. Very upright, very proud and clean, but he used to go through the rubbish in the morning, looking for something he thought he'd lost, and then forget all about it later on in the day. So he'd go out and come back in and it looked to him as if a stranger had come in and strewn rubbish all over his house. He used to say, it was like being haunted by yourself."

"I never know what to say to them," said Alison Grey. "It isn't as though you can tell them it's going to get better. It's not."

"I had a wonderful old lady called Thelma Racket who used to be a psychiatrist, and she knew *exactly* what was happening to her. She hated it. She used to say, 'I never thought this would happen to me.' 'Well,' I said, 'who does, Mrs. Racket?' She had a great sense of humor, but she used to forget which jokes she'd already told me. She was a cyclist when she was younger, she'd even had a unicycle, and every single time I went to care for her she said, 'I used to be a trick cyclist and now I'm turning into a cycle path.' "

"What?" said Alison.

"Trick cyclist, psychiatrist. Cycle path, psychopath."

"Oh, yes!" Alison giggled. "Very good."

"Not when you've heard it a few hundred times," said Sis.

"It's *so* distressing when you see their personality slowly disappearing like that!"

"What's Mr. Alveston like?"

"Oh, very nice, very *good*. He'll be no trouble."

"But what's he *like*?"

"Well, a bit crazy, really."

Sis tutted. Alison was a nice enough woman, but she was so vague. She'd find out for herself about Robert Alveston, though, because now they had arrived at the door and knocked. It was opened by an old gentleman with untidy white hair and no teeth in. Robert had cleaned himself up and done some tidying around the apartment, but the distress of finding his home in such a state had left him half in, half out of the crazies. He'd forgotten about Alison bringing a cleaner to meet him, but he was pleased to see them anyway. He smiled happily at them.

"Ladies!" he exclaimed.

"This is Mrs. Parkinson, come to clean for you," said Alison.

"Oh, dear." Robert turned around to glance into his rooms. "I'm not ready for you yet."

"So pleased to meet you," said Sis, grabbing his hand and shaking it.

Courteously, the old chap bowed his head. "Delighted," he said. "Do come in and please excuse the mess."

The two women stepped inside and Sis cast an expert eye over the state of the place. She'd seen worse. Someone had been at it with a vacuum recently. A bit grubby, but then, old people's houses were often like that. They didn't have the eyesight for the dirt. The only bad thing was a fishy smell, which she was too polite to mention.

"This won't take a minute; it's already almost done," she exclaimed.

Mr. Alveston smiled. "Is it? I must have cleaned it up again. Will you have a cup of tea?"

"Ooh, yes, please. Tea, biscuit, chat, then work, what do you say?"

"He can provide the chat, all right," said Alison. "You'll have to watch him—he's a bit cheeky, this one."

"But I'm over ninety years old!" said Mr. Alveston. And he grinned from ear to ear. He was just delighted with the idea that he was still a bit cheeky.

Sis went to the kitchen to put the kettle on. Alison stood with her papers wrapped in her arms, having a quick chat before she left. Sis was gorgeous. She obviously felt that her job was as much to provide a bit of company for the old things as well as help about the house, and she seemed to like her work, too.

Robert and Sis sat down over the table with tea and chocolate biscuits and told each other about themselves.

Sis came from a large family in which all the women turned out to be great strong things, able to talk one hind leg off a donkey and pull the other off with their bare hands. They lived like tornadoes and died before they reached seventy-five. The men who married these mighty women were all weeds who got bossed about all their lives, went completely senile in their old age, and then carried on to live to enormous ages—ninety-odd in most cases.

Robert told her it was sheer cunning. The men were just letting the women do all the work. Sis said in that case, they paid for their laziness in the end by going crazy.

Robert explained how he had come to end up here in an apartment in Kentish Town, and all alone. He spread his hands and smiled tiredly. "It's like some sort of an accident," he said. "But I can't complain. I've had a wonderful life, but now, well, I'm just waiting to leave it, really."

"Now, don't talk like that!" insisted Sis.

"Oh, I suppose you think I'm feeling sorry for myself, but I'm not. I'm a very old man and there comes a time, with the best will in the world, when you get tired and you just want to stop. There's nothing wrong with that. Everyone has their time to die, it comes to us all, and I've started to look forward to it, that's all. The only problem is, I don't know how to do it. Do you understand, Mrs. Parkinson?"

"Call me Sis," said Sis. She didn't answer. She did understand, and she thought it was wonderful that Mr. Alveston thought like that. But like a lot of people, she found it very hard to talk about such things.

"You'd feel better if you had your family and friends with you," she said. "It sounds to me as if you moved around too much in your life." She told him a story about her cousin who had moved around all over the place, and when her daughter got married, they only had about forty people at the wedding. "Now, me, I've lived here all my life and when *my* daughter got married, we had over THREE HUNDRED GUESTS!" she boasted. She was so pleased with herself that she got up and did a bit of excited dusting before she sat down again.

"Well, I always planned on ending my days here in London, but it's too fast for me now," said Mr. Alveston. "So many people rushing about. I should have stayed in Paris."

"Why don't you move back?"

"Too old. And it's too late. I've been here five

73

years, expecting it to get better, but it hasn't. Sad, isn't it?"

Yes, it was sad, agreed Sis. She looked at him over the top of her glasses. "So how are you managing? You seem very able. Do you have many lapses?"

Robert blushed gently and admitted that yes, he did have lapses. "I came back in just yesterday and the whole place was all topsy-turvy. It looked like some naughty boy had been playing tricks on me and I have no memory at all of having done it."

"Does it happen often?"

"More often lately," he confessed miserably. "The awful thing is, you know you're never going to get any better."

"But that doesn't mean to say it's going to get worse," said Sis.

"In my case, I'm afraid it is."

"Oh, you'll be all right!" exclaimed Sis, but Robert sighed and shook his head.

"Another thing that I *hate*," he said, "is that I'm losing my memories."

"You mean, you're losing your memory?"

"I mean what I say—my *memories*. Oh, I'm losing my memory as well; that's been going on for ages. I can't remember where I put things and so on. But this is different. I do mean memories. Things that happened long ago. Listen: I can't remember who I was when I was a boy." And he looked at her as if he was telling her something of great importance.

"I'm not sure what you mean," said Sis carefully.

"I can't remember who I was! I can't remember my own childhood. Anything! Do you know, I used to spend ages sitting in my chair, dreaming about when I was a lad. But now all my childhood memories are gone. I can still remember what happened to me when I was grown up. I can remember it like it happened yesterday. But my childhood . . . swish! Gone! Kaput!"

"And when did this happen?" asked Sis.

"Five weeks on Thursday," said the old man, with great certainty.

Sis smiled. Mr. Alveston was lovely! He was batty, of course—people didn't lose their memories like that—but it was a strange and beautiful battiness and she loved him for it.

"Your memories will come home," she said, "bringing their tails behind them."

Robert smiled at her. He wasn't being batty. He was telling her the exact and perfect truth. He had lost all his memories of his childhood on the same day and hour and second that he had woken up and seen that strange boy on the floor, who had leapt up into the ventilation grille like a cat. He was only batty enough not to realize how odd it all was.

Sis got up and began to clean the apartment easily with great swooping motions of her muscular arms, while Robert sat on the sofa and watched her, admiring her youth, beauty, and strength. In fact, Sis was neither young nor beautiful, unless you were over ninety years old. But she was certainly strong. She could lift up her husband with one arm and toss pancakes with the other without even sweating.

"Oh, I do like watching people work," teased Mr. Alveston, sitting comfortably in a chair and watching her.

"So long as it's just the work you're watching," said Sis.

"But I'm more than ninety years old!" he said again. He pretended to try and peer up her skirt and Sis said, "It's a good job I put clean underpants on this morning, you old goat."

And Mr. Alveston said, "Yes, red ones, I see." Which made Sis blush, and that made him blush and think he'd overstepped the mark. He went to sit in the bedroom while she finished.

As she'd said, Sis didn't take long. The only unpleasant thing she had to deal with was an old herring that had fallen down the back of the settee, which explained the funny smell. That was nothing.

Some of the other places she had to clean had to be seen to be believed.

Afterward Sis asked Robert if he wanted anything from the shops, but he said he liked to go for himself.

"It's on my way to my other old gentleman, if it's the supermarket you're going to. We could go together," she offered. So he got his coat while Sis had a wash and then the two of them, arm in arm and both of them chattering away like squirrels in a tree, left the apartment and made their way downstairs.

For a few minutes, the apartment was quiet. Then there was a slight scratching noise. The noise got louder, louder. It seemed to be coming from behind the wall. Then quite suddenly a grubby face appeared at the ventilation grille over the armchair.

David had heard everything. He'd been hiding around the corner in the shafts, listening. Now he knew what it meant when his father said that the poor old man was a bit senile. He felt bad about having messed up his place so badly. Poor old man! David had been stupid and cruel, and now he regretted it.

But David shouldn't have come so close to the apartment if he wanted to keep it safe from harm. His presence in the ducts had woken up something else that wasn't at all sorry. As he lay there on his stomach, peering out from behind the grille, he heard something rattling in the kitchen. Quickly David began to creep backward, but it was already too late.

The noise stopped. David felt, rather than heard, a voice in his head. He couldn't quite make it out, so he stopped to listen, and then he heard it, out loud this time. It was as clear as a bell. It was coming from the kitchen.

"Come on!" it said. "Let's wreck it!"

It was the ghost. David froze. He was scared now—not of what it would do to him, but of what it would do to Mr. Alveston's apartment. In the kitchen the rattling began again, louder this time. Things began to fall and break. Then, before his eyes, as he stared at the square of the room framed by the grille, another picture fell off the wall in front of him.

"Don't—stop it!" cried David. He didn't want this to happen! He crawled forward up to the vent, but as he got close a wind of destruction swept around the walls. Pictures fell off one after the other—one, two, three, four, five, six, seven. They cracked as they hit the ground, and a couple of them cracked again as a ghostly foot stamped down on them.

"Stop!" David cried again. He pushed the grille sideways and began to climb down. The breaking stopped as he stood up on the floor and he caught sight of the ghost boy in a corner. The boy's face was twisted with rage; his hands were clenched into fists.

"Let's wreck it!" he screamed.

"Shut up! We'll be heard!" hissed David. He ran through into the kitchen. The fridge door hung open with a wreckage of food tumbling out of it— milk, butter, a little gravy boat with hard white sauce inside, saucers of leftovers, bits of cheese, everything. As he stood and watched, a trickle of milk began to pour itself onto the floor.

David began to put everything back upright, but behind him he heard the tornado start up again. He ran through into the other room in time to see objects flying off the mantelpiece and smashing on the floor.

"Stop it!" he shouted. "What's wrong? Stop it, please stop it!" he yelled.

He couldn't see much of the boy, who seemed to emerge like a blur out of the air here and there around the room, but he caught a couple of good looks at his face. He had a long face, pale as paper.

His mouth was open. His body seemed to be made out of a furious, tearing wind. His expression was poisonous.

"I hate him!" cried the boy. "I hate him!" His face dissolved into tears, and a flurry of destruction whirled around the apartment, breaking out in several places at the same time. David stared in horror at the ornaments breaking and books flying off the walls. The music box cracked down one side and he could see the mechanism glinting dully within. It began to play a horrible, cracked tune.

"Stop it! Just stop!" he shrieked once more. But there was nothing he could do. In tears now, David climbed back into the ducts and crawled back home as fast as he could. Behind him, the ghost screamed at him to come back and play.

"Don't go, don't go!" it screamed. "If you go, I'll get you!" David clenched his teeth and banged forward as fast as he could. A wind began to blow toward him up the ducts, a blast of hot, angry air. Suddenly he was caught in a flurry of papers and photographs that had blown out of the old man's apartment after him. They batted in his face, flicked against his eye—and then he felt a cold, hard hand grab him by the ankle and squeeze until he thought his bones would snap or that the skin would just peel off. With a great push, David fell forward into the duct down toward his own floor. His foot was torn out of the icy grip and he hit the board like a brick. Straightaway he could hear the ghost crashing down right behind him, screaming like a baby and banging like a huge fierce dog in the ducts.

"Don't you leave me! Don't you leave me! I'll get you for this!" it howled. David fell out of the wall into his own apartment, jumped straight back up, and fitted the grille back onto the wall with fumbling fingers. For one dreadful second he saw the face of the ghost boy behind it, twisted with rage like a ball of crumpled paper, its teeth like rows of little shining tusks biting at the grille, before it disappeared like dust before his eyes.

When he got home an hour or so later on, Mr. Alveston was amazed and disgusted. Sis had cleaned up his flat! He'd been there with her when she'd done it! And now look! He'd never seen such a mess.

He must have had another one of his lapses. But when? There hadn't been time. He'd been *out,* for heaven's sake! Was it possible that he'd gone shopping, come home, done all this, and then gone out again just so he could come back and disgust himself like this? It was like Dr. Jekyll and Mr. Hyde. As soon as everything was all cleaned and polished, he'd crept around *behind his own back* and broken everything he could lay his hands on. He could tell it was he who'd done it because he'd picked on all his most precious things—his photographs of Tulip and his wife Greta from Germany and his children—everything that held the fondest memories. No one else would know which things to go for to hurt him the most.

Was he turning into a horrible, stupid old man who didn't care about anything? It was just as if he was being haunted by his own mind. What on earth would Sis say if she knew?

He went to the kitchen and saw the fridge, the mess tumbling out of it as if it had been sick. It was horrible, but another odd thing about it was that he'd started to tidy up again. There were wipe marks on the floor and some of the spilled things had been stood back up the right way. He *must* be mad!

Mr. Alveston got a cloth, got down to the floor, and started to wipe up the mess. Halfway through he suddenly got up on his knees and exclaimed, "But I was *out*!"

But if not him, who? Even though he knew that you shouldn't start believing your own fantasies, he got up and started wandering around the apartment, looking for clues to prove that someone else was doing these awful things. But, of course, he found nothing.

7

A Conversation with the Ghost

That night, David heard crying again. The ghost boy was weeping in a thin, quiet way to itself, as if it didn't know or care if anyone heard it. The sound was clearer and louder than before, as if the ghost was becoming more real every time he went into the ducts. David sat up in bed to listen.

"What's wrong?" whispered David. The ghost didn't answer, but the sobbing became slightly louder. David was sure the boy had heard him.

"Where are you?" David asked again.

The ghost snuffled and a voice from nowhere said, "I'm lost."

"Lost?" David was puzzled. He looked around and tried to work out where the voice was coming from. "Where do you want to go?" he asked.

"I don't know, I'm lost."

"Well, where do you belong, then?"

"Sod that," hissed the ghost. David laughed. A swearing ghost! The ghost laughed back.

"Sod that!" said the voice, and this time David could place it. It was coming from the floor by the side of his bed, and when he turned to look, there was the ghost lying there. He was on his side toward the wall, but he had twisted his head around so that David could see his wide, tearstained face breaking out into a laugh as he looked up at him. The face got bigger, and at first David thought he was sitting up, but it wasn't that. His face was simply getting bigger, wider, closer. Maybe it was just the ghost's way of getting closer to him, but it made David cry out in fright. Then the laugh faded, and the figure faded with it, and all David could make out was a paleness in the place where the ghost had sat.

"I'm here now," said the voice softly, and David almost jumped out of bed in fright, because suddenly the voice wasn't coming from the floor by his bed, but from behind the grille leading to the ducts. There was a pause and then the voice said clearly, "Come in here with me."

David felt a thrill of fear go up his spine. Go in there—into the night with a ghost? He shook his head.

"Why do you want me to go in there?"

"We can get that old guy."

"Who are you? What's your name?"

"I don't have a name," said the ghost.

"You must have a name."

"No name!"

The ghost sounded angry, so David said, "I'll call you Charlie, then."

"That's not my real name."

The voice seemed to be moving about and it was making David feel odd, trying to talk to someone who only had a shape sometimes. He turned his bedside light on, slipped out of bed, and went to the ducts to peer in. He couldn't see anything.

"Where *are* you?" he hissed.

"Here. Sometimes." The ghost laughed. "Sometimes I'm here and sometimes I'm somewhere else. Come inside. You'll be able to see me if you come in."

"Somewhere else where?"

"Somewhere that's not here."

"Is that where you come from?"

"I used to be with the others."

"What others?"

"I don't know. The others."

"Where were you with the others?"

"I don't know."

David was getting cross. The ghost's answers didn't tell him anything—no name, no place, nothing.

"What do you want me for?"

"It's lonely in here. I want you to play with me."

"I don't like your games," said David anxiously, remembering what had happened in the old man's apartment.

The ghost laughed. David thought he could see it again. He peered into the gloom. "I didn't like what you did to that apartment."

"I hate him! He's evil. He's old. He wants to get me!"

"He wants to get you? Why?"

"He wants me, he wants me inside him, but he won't get me."

"What, do you think he wants to eat you? That's nuts."

"You don't know. Come in here with me."

"No."

"Please. It's scary on my own. We can be friends. Come in . . ."

"I'm tired. I have school tomorrow. I . . ."

"You should do as I say. I could get you like I get him. You . . ."

"No!" shouted David in fear. He stepped back from the ducts and the ghost shrieked as if he had just caused it an unearthly pain. In a flash before his eyes he saw the creature again. Something had gone wrong. Its hands were reaching forward, holding on to the grille, and its body stretched out behind as if some unearthly force was blowing it back into the ductwork. It didn't want to go; it was hanging on as hard as it could. Its mouth was open and yelling, but David couldn't hear anything. He could see the white clear fingers on the bars, he could see the face perfectly clearly. He could even feel the ghost's cold breath, which smelled of dust and cold metal.

David leapt up with a cry, half wanting to run, half wanting to help, but in the next moment the force got too strong and the boy blew away. He could hear the ghostly body bumping and swirling down the ducts as he was rushed away deep into the building.

Everything went quiet. About ten seconds later he heard the weeping again. It went on for a minute or two, then it stopped. David heard nothing more for the rest of the night.

8

The Quick Mind of Sis Parkinson

On Thursday afternoon Sis Parkinson came by to do housework for Mr. Alveston again. She liked the old man. She thought it was a complete gas that he pretended to look up her skirt and see what color underwear she had on, although both of them would really have been mortified if he ever actually did see. He'd lived an interesting life, he was funny, knew a little about everything and a lot about some things. He was good company.

He reminded Sis of a naughty boy trapped in an old, old body. When she'd walked him to the shops last time, he'd held on to her elbow trembling like a leaf, he was so fragile.

"What's it like being old?" she'd asked him.

"I don't feel any different from when I was ten. It's just that everything's so *worn out*," he told her.

This time she brought along a bottle of red wine and some salted nuts and other snacks in her bag. She was thinking that when she'd finished the cleaning, she'd get out a couple of glasses and put the nuts in little bowls, and she and Mr. Alveston could sit and get tipsy together before she went home. Do him a world of good—and her, too.

I could fancy him if he was forty or fifty years younger, she thought as she waited for the elevator. Or if I was fifty years older, she thought, and she roared out loud with laughter at such a thought, just as the door opened and a middle-aged woman clutching a poodle in her arms dashed out. She looked at Sis as if she was mad for standing there on her own, roaring with laughter.

I like being a bit kooky myself, thought Sis.

But when she got to Mr. Alveston's, her good mood disappeared.

The old man was gray and ill looking, a shadow of himself. He'd aged years over two days. He peeped anxiously at her from the doorway and told her he wouldn't be needing her today, but when she looked past him into the apartment, the place had been utterly pulled to pieces. It took her five minutes before he gave up with a useless gesture and let her in. He sat down at the table, looking down at his wrinkled hands. He was trembling so much more than last time. He hadn't shaved. He was still in his pajamas and looked, if Sis knew anything about it, depressed.

"What's the matter, love, what is it?"

"Nothing, nothing," he told her.

Sis stuck her lip out. "Are you having one of your lapses, Robert?" she asked him, and he said, "I just don't know, Sis. I don't seem to know what I'm doing at the moment, I don't."

Sis looked around the apartment. She'd never seen such a mess. She opened her bag and took out the bottle of wine. The apartment would have to wait. People before tidiness, that was her motto.

Mr. Alveston was so distressed and scared about what was happening that he didn't want to talk about it—he was sure they'd put him away if they found out. But once Sis got him going, out it all came. Poor old man! No wonder he was in such a state. He was wrecking his own apartment without even knowing he was doing it!

"That's a funny sort of lapse," said Sis.

"I just can't work out when I did it," he told her. "I mean, we were out, weren't we? I was having a good day. I thought I could remember every second of what I did when we were out. But I must have come and wrecked everything and then gone out again and then come home again. . . . It seems so . . . so deliberate. It's as if I was being two people at once. That's not just going crazy, is it, Sis? It's going completely bananas. I don't want to go mad. It's so unfair. After living more than ninety years, you'd think going mad wouldn't be a problem, would it?"

"Of course you're not going mad," said Sis, although she wasn't really so sure. "If you were going to go crazy you'd have done it years ago. Now, what else has been going on?"

Mr. Alveston told the rest of his tale. He was hearing voices. He was seeing things. He'd seen a boy in the ventilation system, for instance.

"A boy? In the ventilation system?"

"Yes," admitted Mr. Alveston, and he looked at Sis from the corners of his eyes to see how she reacted. It was the first time he'd told anyone about that and even though he knew it was ridiculous, he would have just loved Sis to jump up and say that it was all true.

Sis turned around to look at the grille on the wall and then back to stare at him.

"Well," she said.

"It would explain everything," said Mr. Alveston. "Do you see? There's some children found their way in and it's not me, it's them. It's them coming in to do all these horrible things. Do you see? Sis?"

Oh, dear. It was worse than she thought. Once they started inventing fantasies to explain what was happening to them, they were quite well gone. And once they started believing them—well. Dear, oh, dear, it looked as though Alison was right. He'd have to go in a home after all.

"It's possible," insisted Mr. Alveston. He was beginning to babble. "They'd know when I go out and when I come in. They could be in there *now*. They could be listening to everything we say."

Dear, oh dear, oh dear.

"Yes, well, of course it's possible," said Sis carefully. "Stranger things have happened, I know. Only it's not very *likely*, is it?"

"I knew it—I *am* going mad!" wailed the poor old man. He put his face in his hands and wept, and Sis's heart melted away for him.

"It's the home for me, isn't it, Sis? I'm not safe anymore, am I?"

"Well," she said practically, "the first thing to do is find out if it is true or not, then we can worry about what's going on in there." She tapped his poor old head. "Now, drink up your wine"—and she picked hers up and gulped it down—"and let's have a look behind that grille."

She put down her glass and went over to the grille, with Mr. Alveston tottering along behind her. He was such a frail little old thing that she had to be careful not to dash and jump about in case she knocked him down. She got a chair and put it against the wall, and climbed up to have a look in.

"The grille comes off easily; it just slides out," said Sis. "Have you got a flashlight?" she asked, but Mr. Alveston was already running off to fetch it.

The yellow beam poked a long bright finger down the duct. There was nothing to be seen but patches of dust and dirt, but that was what attracted her attention. It was the sort of thing someone who does a lot of cleaning would notice. The duct should have been either dusty all over or clean all over, but this one had little triangles and scrapes of greasy dust left here and there, just as if someone had been wriggling their way along and wiped most of the dust off onto themselves as they went by.

"Well, that's very odd," said Sis. She got down off the chair and examined the wall under the grille. Sure enough, there were smudges and marks on the wallpaper. Now that she thought about it, she remembered rubbing several black marks with a damp cloth off the wall the last time she was there.

Sis dashed across to the table and took a long swig of wine. Mr. Alveston was standing there, playing with his pajama cord and looking nervously at her, but she didn't say anything yet. She didn't want to raise his hopes. Maybe it was he who had wiped the mess off the inside of the ducts and onto the wall, who knew?

But she was on the trail now. She sat the old man down and set off down the hall outside the apartment, knocking on doors and seeing if anyone else had heard or seen anything strange. It was afternoon, most of the neighbors were out at work, but she did find some people who were able to help. Two doors along was a young man called Malcolm who worked nights. He told her that yes, he had heard all sorts of odd noises coming from the ducts. He'd thought they were doing some sort of work in the building, weren't they?

Farther along she found a middle-aged woman who'd taken early retirement. "Oh, yes. We hear all sorts going on," she said. "It's noises coming in from the other apartments, you see. You get to hear all sorts—I don't think people realize just how far noises carry in the ducts. Sometimes it's so clear, you could swear you were in the same room. It's fascinating. Arguments, fights, people falling in and out of love, all sorts of things. You can never *quite* make out what people are saying, though. There are times I wish I could shrink myself down to half size so I could get in and have a good listen. Just the other afternoon I heard the most awful *screams*. Dreadful. I was very concerned."

"What happened?"

"They stopped." The woman smiled vaguely and Sis thought, Well, you should have done something.

Farther down the hall she found an old woman who lived with her three cats and a parrot called Philbert. She had to put a cover over the parrot's cage whenever anyone came to knock at the door because he swore in the most disgusting fashion. It was the old woman who'd taught him to swear, and she was always looking for new words to teach him. But she was a kind old lady who only did it to amuse herself.

"Oh, so that's what it is," she said. "I'd forgotten about the old ducts. I had them blocked up in my apartment. Yes, there've been all sorts of odd noises coming through the walls lately. It sounds like some-one crawling around in there. Especially on Tues-days and Thursdays, for some reason," she added.

"Right," said Sis. "Thank you for your help."

And on the next floor down, Sis found a teacher who was having a day off, and who'd found some odd things happening. It had started with a boot missing, the left one. Then the following week, the boot had come back and the right one was gone—along with her remote control for the TV and a few other things.

"Can you remember what day it was when these things went missing?" asked Sis. After some thought, Mary said it had happened at the beginning of the week, Tuesday perhaps.

Sis went back to Mr. Alveston and told him what she'd found out. Then she did the housework. She was as cross as a rhinoceros.

9

The Second Ghost

Being haunted wasn't at all what David had expected it to be. Now he knew why people were so scared of ghosts. It was because ghosts were so full of fear themselves. All that fear made this ghost dangerous. What did he want? Who was he and what was his real name? Ghosts are mystery stories. Where did he come from, and why was he haunting Mahogany Villas? The clue to the whole thing seemed to be the old man, Mr. Alveston. What had the ghost to do with him, and why did he hate him so much?

Over the next few days, David thought about

these questions, but he had no answers. At night, he listened for the mysterious voice or the sound of weeping in the ducts, but he heard nothing at all. Perhaps the ghost had gone to rest.

It was a Tuesday afternoon. David knew what was going to happen as soon as he got home from school.

I'm not going in, he told himself. Then he said it aloud. "I'm not going in!" Silence answered him, but it was a silence with someone in it.

David drank some juice and turned on the TV, but all the time he was aware of the dark space behind the wall calling him. Soon he found himself listening through the babble from the TV, trying to make out a whisper that he was sure was coming from the ducts. He couldn't make it out, but he felt if only he got just a little closer, or perhaps if he just got a little bit inside the ducts, he'd be able to hear what the ghost boy wanted to tell him. He did his best, but it was just too tempting.

"Just . . . oh, all right, then!" he snapped. And he got up, pushed the sofa to the wall, and put his head close to the vent. He held his breath and listened. That whisper! It was there, it was calling him, but he still couldn't quite make it out. . . .

"I'm not coming in," he said grumpily, but there was no answer.

David went back to watch more TV, but it was no use. Within another five minutes he'd changed out of his school clothes, slid back the grille, and was inside with the ghost.

"Just for a bit, then," he whispered.

He could feel the ghost inside there, everywhere. He couldn't see him, but he was there—in the darkness, in the cool air, everywhere. David began to move along the duct toward Mary's flat, but the ghost didn't want that.

"Not here," the air whispered to him. "Not there. Up, up. Go up!"

And although he knew there was trouble in the air, David did what the ghost wanted. He began to wriggle his way backward toward the up duct. All around him, he could feel the wicked glee of the ghost. He was scared; maybe they were going to do something really bad this time. A trap for Mr. Alveston? Trip wires, something falling on his head when he opened the door? He'd have to make sure nothing like that happened.

David had made his way up to the fifth floor and begun to creep along the duct toward Mr. Alveston's apartment when he heard the noise behind him. It was a rattling, banging noise, far away but getting rapidly closer. David froze in fear.

"What's that?" he hissed.

Someone else didn't like it, either. All around him, David could feel the fear. The little ghost was terrified out of his wits.

"What is it?" David cried, but the ghost said nothing. David lifted himself up on his toes and hands and looked backward between his legs. The noise was shooting up toward them, fast as a cat running through the ducts. Then something hard suddenly struck the board that David had put over the duct on the floor below. There was a clatter as the board was knocked off, and then the rattle, louder than ever, carried up toward them.

The ghost screamed and fled. David felt it rushing up the duct ahead of him. He screamed himself and followed, but he could only go at a slow crawl, trapped on his belly as he was. The thing was coming after them and it was almost there! What was it—another ghost? Something from hell come to take the ghost back? Panting and sweating, David dragged himself along. The most awful thing was not being able to look behind, and by the time he got to the duct that led to Mr. Alveston's apartment, he couldn't bear it anymore. He stopped, lifted himself up on his toes and fingers, and looked back, shining the flashlight between his legs. He was just in time to see something terrible emerging from the duct down.

It was made out of something thin and hard—bone, David thought. A skeleton was coming—a horrible, thin arm bone reaching out from the duct. It was blocking the way down.

With another loud scream, David hurtled down the duct toward Mr. Alveston's apartment. He was screaming and screaming. The grille was off, thank God. He pushed his head out and a pair of strong hands grabbed him by the shoulders. He screamed again. It had him! He was dragged out of the duct and crashed down to the floor, but he was on his feet again in a flash. He ran for the door, but someone was in the way. He hurled himself at the figure, but he just bounced back.

He pointed at the vent and howled, "It's coming! Let me out, it's coming!"

Mr. Alveston appeared from the bedroom. "It's all in the mind, boy—in the mind," he said, tapping his head as if he knew all about it.

A big woman was standing over David. "Now, then—what's been going on?" she demanded.

10

Trapped

David made another break for the door, but he was trapped. Still in a panic, he backed away from the vent in the wall. Sis Parkinson was standing by the door, growling. Mr. Alveston blinked dimly at him.

"Where's the boy gone?" David demanded.

"Oh, so there's another one in it, is there?" demanded Sis. "What's his name? Come on!"

"He's not a boy, he's a ghost!" But one look at her face and David knew it was no use. No one was going to believe him. As he'd thought, he was going to take the blame—all of it.

"Ghosts don't drink and they don't pee," pointed out Mr. Alveston. He began to giggle at the thought, but Sis was getting more annoyed by the second.

"You horrible, selfish little . . . ," she began, but they were interrupted by a banging on the door. It was the janitor.

The whole thing was a setup. Sis had worked it all out. The marks in the duct and on the wall told her that something funny was going on; the old lady a few doors down, and Mary, had told her that Tuesdays and Thursdays were the days funny things happened. It had to be a child getting in through the duct because no adult would be small enough. That meant that the most likely time for things to happen would be after school hours on Tuesday or Thursday afternoons.

She and Mr. Alveston had waited in the living room to hear if any noises came. When they did, she alerted the janitor over her cell phone. He had run down to the basement, where he had one of those long, jointed, bendy poles people use to stick up chimneys, and he'd shoved it up into the ventilation system, length after length of it, right up to the fifth floor. It was this pole snaking its way up that David had heard banging and crashing its way up the ducts, and the same pole that had lifted the board behind him and cast that bony shadow on the duct and thrown him into a blind panic.

It was, as Mr. Alveston said, all in the mind.

"You're in the worst sort of trouble," hissed Sis. She was barely able to keep her hands off the little swine.

"What sort of trouble?" asked David.

"Police trouble! I hope they lock you up and throw away the key. I hope they spend the rest of your life ferrying you about from home to home. I hope they put you into foster care! I hope . . ."

"But what about the ghost?" wailed David. "I heard it. It made me do things."

Sis had been hissing like a basket of vipers, and now she simply blew up. "You're just a nasty little piece of work," she yelled. She rushed across the room and started making strange passes with her hands around his head. What she wanted to do, very badly, was to hit him. But as someone employed by the social services, she knew that if you hit a child, you were in bad trouble, so she just had to attack the air around him instead.

After that, the janitor called the optician's and got David's dad away from work to deal with David, and all hell broke loose all over again, with his dad yelling, "How could you, how could you, how could you!" and begging forgiveness from Mr. Alveston. Fortunately for David, Mr. Alveston was by now utterly exhausted after all the fuss and asked everyone to leave so he could get a little sleep.

Outside the door, David, his dad, Sis, and the janitor walked along to the elevator.

"Of course the police will have to be informed," Sis told Terry stiffly.

"Is that necessary?"

"Of course it's bloody necessary, what do you think?" she yelled.

Terry paled before her. "Can't we do social workers and things?" he asked.

"Police. Social workers. Capital punishment! Anything! All of it! Just keep the little toad out of my sight! And if you're any sort of father, you'll *beat* him till he can't sit down!"

Sis, unable to stand still any longer, stormed off down the hall to the stairway. Terry smiled weakly at the janitor, but the janitor was unsympathetic.

"She's right, mate. Face it, he could have killed the poor old guy." Then he walked off as well. Alone, David and his dad caught the elevator down to the next floor and let themselves in the apartment. In the living room was the telltale grille, lying on the floor next to the sofa David had used to climb up.

"Sorry, Dad," said David. His dad didn't reply. Later, as he was washing up after dinner, David was horrified to see that his dad was crying.

It didn't stop there, of course. Later on, the police turned up.

"Breaking and entering and vandalism, just for firsts," said the policeman viciously.

"Will I go to prison?" David asked.

"I certainly hope so," said the policeman. Then he arrested him.

Next day the social worker, Alison Grey, came by to see what "support" David needed to get over his problem. They had a long chat about caring for others, about responsibility, and on and on. There was a lot of talk from his dad about David being bullied at school. Alison was sympathetic.

"Aren't you mad?" David asked her.

"Well, I am, of course. It was a horrible thing to do. But it's my job to help, you see. Punishment isn't my thing. That's the police, isn't it?"

It wasn't going to be over soon, either. There were going to be social workers' reports. There were going to be tests. Then when all the reports were in, there would be a court case.

David's dad was beside himself with worry. He didn't know what to do, or what to think, or what to feel. All he knew was that he was desperately concerned for his boy. He was sure it was all his fault. He'd been moping about the place, not going out, not making friends, not getting a new woman in his life, as if his life had ended when his wife left home. What a pain he must be to live with! No wonder David was getting into trouble.

A couple of nights later, he crept up to his son's bedroom to peep in and see if David was sleeping properly. It was very late; he'd already been to bed himself, but he couldn't sleep for worry.

He crept up to the door, which was ajar, and he heard whispering. He peeped in.

David was standing on a chair below the grille to the ventilation shaft. He was talking to the shaft, but Terry couldn't hear any answers. The one-sided conversation went something like this.

"I told you, I don't want to," said David.

"Not anymore," said David.

"I bet you can't do it on your own," said David.

"Don't talk like that!" David almost shouted.

"You can't make me. Just leave him alone!" David cried.

"Oh my God, he's talking to himself," said Terry. Unable to stop himself, even though he thought it was the wrong thing to do, he opened the door and ran in. David leapt off his chair in one great bound.

"What's going on?" begged Terry.

"Nothing!"

"Nothing? You're talking to the ventilation shaft!"

"It's just a game."

"What do you mean, a game?"

"It's a game. I tell it things," lied David.

"What sort of things?"

"Secrets!"

"Secrets? But it was talking back to you!"

"Did you hear it?"

"No, but the way you were talking . . . Oh, David, what's going *on*?"

"I'm sorry, I'm sorry, Dad. I'll be all right, I'll be all right. Don't worry."

Terry took him back to bed and lay next to him for a while. He felt devastated. David lay awkwardly by his side. Later, when his son was asleep, Terry crept into the living room, stood on a chair, and listened to the ventilation system himself, but he could hear nothing but the wind stirring inside the building and the dull mutterings and murmurings coming up from other people's apartments.

• • •

Next thing, David's dad decided that they needed to make friends with the old man. He was the one who had suffered. If he decided that David was all right, that it was a onetime thing, maybe the police wouldn't press charges.

Sis Parkinson had told David to stay well away from Mr. Alveston, and so had the social worker, Alison. But Terry caught the old boy in the lobby one day. Mr. Alveston wasn't keen at first. He was so frail that he was no match for a boy, even a little one. But he agreed to accept a visit from David to say he was sorry so long as Terry came along as well.

David didn't fancy the idea. He hadn't forgotten that maybe the old man was a murderer, even though he felt sorry for him now. Who knew what he had been like when he was young? There was still the mystery of why the ghost boy was haunting him. But Terry insisted, so the next day after school, David and his dad turned up with chocolates, wine, and flowers and an invitation for dinner the next night.

The old man opened the door and stood there watching quietly. He was so old, it was almost impossible to imagine. David thought he was creepy. He fumbled his way through his apology with his dad standing close behind him. It was difficult to tell what such an old man was feeling. He accepted the presents and the invitation. Then he pointed behind David's back, and when David turned around to have a look, he stamped on his toe with his walking stick as hard as he could.

"That's for scaring me. See you tomorrow," shouted the old man, and he slammed the door in David's face. It was agony. David hopped about yelling and howling. He could hear Mr. Alveston laughing at him from behind the door.

David's dad was pleased.

"Aha, he's made a mistake now. That's assault on a minor. He'll have to drop the charges now or we can get *him* arrested!"

"But that's not fair!" protested David.

"No, but it's nice to have it up your sleeve just in case, don't you think?" asked Terry.

The next day when the old man turned up for dinner he apologized for hurting David—he explained that he just wanted his revenge, which David could understand.

The old man sat at the table, trembling like a newly hatched chick. David couldn't believe that he had been so mean to him. Mr. Alveston was so frail, you felt that you had to tiptoe past him. If you bumped into him, he might break or fall over and not be able to get back up.

"Only a few more years and you'll be a hundred and get a telegram from the Queen, Mr. Alveston," said Terry.

The old man smiled. "I hope not," he said in his soft, quavering voice.

"Don't you want a telegram from the Queen?" asked David.

"Oh, I don't care about that. But I don't want to be so old. I don't like being as old as I am."

"It's better than the alternative," said Terry. He meant, being dead. He smiled weakly.

"Do you think so? But I'm very tired. Everyone wants to live forever, but nobody likes old age." The old man smiled at David. "But how could you understand? You're so young. When you get as old as I am, things change."

David was fascinated by this conversation. "But don't you want to be a hundred?" he asked.

"No, no, I don't. I've had everything I want out of life. You know, David, everyone tells you how to live, but no one ever tells you how to die. All the people I knew when I was young have already died. Even most of the people I knew when I was an old man have died. Now that I'm such a very, very old man, I would like to go and join them."

A stillness settled around the table. Terry toyed with his fork. No one ever talked about such things.

"Do you believe in heaven?" David wanted to know.

"No. When I say I want to join them, it's just a way of talking. People don't like to talk about dying, so they say 'pass on,' 'go to join my loved ones.' But look, we're disturbing your father." Mr. Alveston twinkled. He seemed to quite like shocking people. "You're young, you don't have to worry about such things. I have all my life behind me. You have all yours ahead of you. Let's not talk of death, I've punished you enough. Now, I have a question for you. What made you go inside those ventilation ducts?"

". . . I don't know."

"It must be very dark in there. Not a good place to play."

David stared at him. He'd been asked that question before—by his father, by the police, by the social worker. Even his mum, Topsy, had asked him about it when she called him a few days before. There wasn't one of them he could tell the truth to. A ghost! What would that be to them? An excuse he was making, perhaps. Or they'd think he was going mad. Perhaps he was.

But now, looking at this old man, who was tired of this world and thinking about the next, who knew so much about being alive that he could even want to die, David thought it might be possible to tell him. What would he think? But Terry was there, listening, so David just shrugged and said again that he didn't know.

He had a chance later on, though, when his dad went out to make custard for the pudding.

"Mr. Alveston," he said. "Do you believe in ghosts?"

Mr. Alveston looked at him with his trembling eye. "Why should I believe in ghosts?" he said.

"Because I saw one. In the ducts. There's a ghost in the ducts."

"What sort of ghost?"

"A boy like me."

The old man thought carefully about it. "Are you sure it wasn't just the darkness playing tricks on you?"

"I saw him! I talked to him. He's in there now." David nodded at the vent on the wall.

"Ghosts," said Mr. Alveston. He smiled. "Are you asking me because you think that I might soon be one myself?"

David thought about it. "You don't seem to get very old ghosts," he said.

Mr. Alveston laughed. "No! It's true. You never do. Ghosts on canes! Ghosts with false teeth!" He sat in his chair and wheezed slightly with laughter. "Well, at least I'll never haunt anyone. I've used up all my time on this earth," he said.

"Have you ever seen a ghost?" asked David.

"Children are always interested in ghosts. Well, yes, perhaps I have. There have been occasions when I've thought I might have seen a ghost. And do you know what I thought? I thought, maybe the ghost was like a memory. Do you see? We have memories all around us. When you play music on a tape, it's a memory of people playing music. When you put a video on, it's a memory of people talking and moving. People are very much more wonderful than machines. Perhaps we play back our memories sometimes without meaning to. Or perhaps, we play back other people's memories without meaning to. If you see a memory being played back, that's a ghost. Do you see?"

David wasn't sure if he did. His dad came in with the Swiss roll and custard. "Then it would do the same thing over and over again, wouldn't it?"

"I don't know. Human beings are very much more wonderful than machines," repeated the old man. He smiled at Terry. "Your son has some interesting things to say."

"Has he?" said Terry. Truth to tell, that was something David's dad had never noticed.

Mr. Alveston began to eat his pudding, but halfway through he put his spoon down and sat there staring at his bowl. When David asked him another question, he didn't answer.

"Mr. Alveston? Mr. Alveston?" asked David.

"What?" he said.

"It's me—David. Mr. Alveston?"

"I'm . . . very tired. Very tired. I think it's time for me to go home." He looked at David and frowned, as if he wasn't sure what was happening or where he was.

Terry got him his coat and helped him into it. Before he went, Mr. Alveston turned to David and looked at him gravely. "You gave me a terrible fright, you know," he said. "I thought I was going mad."

"Me too," said David.

After he had walked the old man home, Terry congratulated his son.

"You talked to him," he said. "You had a conversation."

"So what?"

"A proper conversation. You only ever grunt at me. Why do I never get a proper conversation?"

"What?"

"I'd like you to talk to me sometimes. Instead of just *at* me like you usually do. Amazing. A proper conversation!" Terry hadn't realized how long it was since he and David had just chatted about things. He felt jealous. "A proper conversation!" he repeated.

"Shut up."

The next day there was a note through the door, thanking them for the meal and asking if David would like to stop by for a chat sometimes.

"You can stop by for some chores sometimes, more like," said his dad.

"Okay," said David.

11

Friends

Over the next few weeks, nearly all of David's spare time was used up. Every Wednesday after school he had to go to see the child psychologist. Every Friday, Alison Grey, the social worker, came to see him. Things got better at school, because the teachers found out what had happened at home and started to watch out for the bullying. With all that attention, David began to feel a lot better about life. There were still the police hanging over the whole thing, though.

And the ghost. Was he still there, hiding behind the walls? After he had been caught, David had heard the ghost weeping a couple of times. Other times, he could sense him waiting for him to come and speak to him. He'd tried to ignore it, but in the end he'd had to go and talk to him. That was the conversation Terry had heard him have. The ghost had been trying to get him back to the old man's apartment.

"I told you, I don't want to," David had said.

The ghost had said that David used to like going in there with him.

"Not anymore," David had said.

The ghost said that unless David came with him, he'd do something really bad.

"I bet you can't do it on your own," David had said.

The ghost had said, "I'll kill him. Or I'll kill you."

"Don't talk like that!" David had said.

"You've got to come," the ghost had said.

"You can't make me. Just leave him alone!" David had said.

David was terrified that the ghost really would hurt poor old Mr. Alveston. Maybe he really could kill him. And what would happen to David then?

In the end, the problem was solved for him. A couple of days later he came home from school and found a workman on a ladder in the front room plastering over where the duct had been. The opening had been bricked up, and so had the one in his bedroom. Later on, he discovered that the openings into Mr. Alveston's apartment had been blocked up, too.

David wondered what it would be like in there for the ghost now. Was he trapped in there forever? He wasn't sure that bricks and plaster were enough to keep a ghost away if it wanted to come in, but that night, and the night after that, and the night after that, the soft weeping and breathy voice of the ghost didn't disturb his sleep. David began to hope that the ghost was out of his life for good.

Two or three times a week he went to see old Mr. Alveston, to do some vacuuming or shopping or to make him a cup of tea. His dad made it clear he had to, but in fact he quite enjoyed it. You never knew what Mr. Alveston was going to be like. He had lived such an impossibly long time, he was full of stories and ideas. You never knew whether he was going to be boring, fascinating, quiet, clever, or just plain nuts.

Once he was making a fish cake for his supper, and he did it with flour, sugar, currants, and chopped lemon peel with a couple of tins of sardines stirred in.

David was mesmerized. He'd never heard of anything like it. Mr. Alveston smiled reassuringly at him as he stirred in the sardines, and David smiled back in wonder. Perhaps this was something they used to do years and years ago. It wasn't until the cake was done and in the oven baking away that Mr. Alveston realized what he'd done.

"What's that funny smell?" he asked. "It smells like someone's put fish in a fruit cake."

"Well, we just did!" said David, and he began howling with laughter. But poor Mr. Alveston looked so sad, he had to stop. That was the first time he realized what everyone meant when they said that Mr. Alveston was getting a bit strange.

"Another lapse," he said, throwing the cake in the trash. "Oh, well, one of us enjoyed it, David."

Other times weren't so much fun. He once found Mr. Alveston opening all the jars in his cupboard, looking for something he'd lost. What it was that was lost, he couldn't make out. David helped him look, even though the old man was calling him Simon. Mr. Alveston was scraping out the marmalade with his fingers, shaking tea and coffee onto the floor, and then combing through the mess with his fingers. His eyes had gone shiny and starey.

David helped for a bit, then he excused himself and went to get his dad. Terry gently helped Mr. Alveston up and got him cleaned up, but it upset

David terribly to see the old man in such a state, not knowing who or where he was or what was going on around him. The next day, he was back to normal.

"I'm as bad as your ghost," he said sadly when David told him what had happened. It was becoming obvious to everyone, even him, that he couldn't stay living on his own for much longer.

They often talked about the ghost. Mr. Alveston had stories of his own. There was one from the time he'd lived in a house in Sydney, Australia, where something pale started to go for a walk across the hall of his house every evening at eight.

"It came out of the wall on one side, crossed the hallway, and then went straight through the wall at the other side, every single night for a week," he said. "In the end we found out that another house stood on the same spot long ago, so I suppose the ghost was still following where the hallway of the old one used to be."

He had another story about a dog that used to bark at something in the corner when there was no one there, and another when he was wandering in a garden late at night when something grabbed his ankle.

"But when I put my hand down to my foot, there

was nothing there," he said. He had to stand there for about ten or twenty seconds before whatever it was let him go, with no harm done.

"That's one thing about ghosts; they never seem to hurt anyone," he pointed out.

But even he, long though he had lived, had no stories to match David's. A ghost that talked, a ghost that smashed the place to bits, a ghost that had a face. Who had ever heard of such a thing?

David had no idea how much of his own story Mr. Alveston believed, but, kind old gent that he was, he had more than forgiven David; he liked him. He put in a word with the police. He pointed out that David came to visit him often, helped with his shopping and other chores. The police decided not to take it any further. They let David off with a warning. Everything was going so well, and then came the phone call.

It was seven o'clock Wednesday evening when the call came. Terry and David were having their dinner. David knew at once that something was wrong. Then his dad dropped the phone and made long steps to the door.

"What is it?" he begged.

"Mr. Alveston—he's taken a fall."

Father and son raced up the stairs. The door was

locked; they could hear the old man crying weakly on the other side. Terry had the key in his pocket—Mr. Alveston had given him one for just such a time as this—and opened the door swiftly.

It was a disaster. The place had been trashed.

They found Mr. Alveston lying on the floor in the kitchen; his skin looked like ash and there was blood on his face and hands. He was shaking. He wept with pain when Terry helped him to a chair in the living room. The apartment had been destroyed. There wasn't a picture left on the wall, not a book left in the cases, not an ornament or vase in one piece. Even the furniture had been wrecked. There was barely a stick left in one piece. The floor was covered in broken china and glass, the drawers emptied, the stove hissing gas. Terry sniffed the air and hurriedly turned it off. The table was overturned, the fridge lay on its side. David understood two things at once. One, the ghost was back. Two, he was going to get the blame.

"It wasn't me," he said to his dad.

"It wasn't him," agreed the old man.

Terry was already on the phone calling for an ambulance. "Do you know that for sure?" he asked over his shoulder.

"Yes, I'm certain the boy who did it was still here when I came in," said Mr. Alveston.

123

Terry turned back to the phone, called the ambulance, and, with a funny glance at his son, the police. While he was busy, Mr. Alveston called David over. He gripped the boy by his shoulder and stared wildly at him.

"I saw him—your ghost. He came in here like the Furies! I thought he was going to kill me, David."

"Thank you—thank you," said David. He was so relieved, and so shocked at the same time. He put his arms carefully around Mr. Alveston, squeezed as hard as he dared, and began to cry.

12

The Closed Door

"The dirty, cunning little sneak. What a *toad*! Coming in and making himself at home. Being friendly. Being nice. Getting himself off the hook. Oh, what a little angel! And then as soon as everything's sorted out, in he comes with his horrible vandal friends and wrecks the whole place. It's disgusting. He ought to be locked away!"

Sis Parkinson and Alison Grey were standing in the ruins of Mr. Alveston's apartment. Neither of them had ever seen such a mess.

"You don't think Mr. Alveston could have done it himself, do you?" said Alison Grey weakly. "They do sometimes, you know." She'd grown to like David over the past few weeks. She'd thought he was friends with the old man. It was a terrible shock to her faith in human nature to think that the boy had come in and done something like this.

Sis had tears in her eyes. "How *could* he?" she demanded.

The furniture was upended. A leg had been torn off the coffee table and stabbed through the TV screen. A metal desk lamp had been bent almost double. Drawers had been wrenched out and flung all over, their contents scattered like rubbish. It looked as though some terrible force of nature, the kind of thing you found in deserts or ravines or in the ocean depths, had let itself loose in there. How could an old man nearly one hundred years old have done anything like it?

"If Mr. Alveston did it, he must have some sort of potion he takes when he wants to rip furniture to pieces. I wish I had some of it, that's all," said Sis.

Alison winced. David had seemed a nice boy! "But could a child of twelve do it, either? Look at this!" She picked up the table lamp and tried to straighten it over her knee. It didn't budge. "I can't do it, let alone a child."

Carelessly, Sis took the lamp from Alison and twisted it back into shape with one jerk of her hands.

"He had an accomplice," she said. "A bigger boy. A teenager! That must be the lad Mr. Alveston saw."

"But he was doing so well! Everyone said so. At school. At home. His father . . ."

"That wimp!"

"The reports from the child psychologist were super."

"Psychologists! Excuse me, I've nothing against social services, Alison, but what that lad wants isn't the chance to sit down and talk about himself for hours on end, but a good hard slipper across his backside, that's what he wants."

The doorbell rang. Alison picked her way across the debris while Sis began sorting out books from the rubbish.

It was David and his dad.

Sis heard their voices and came storming over. "You!" she yelled. "Worming your way into his affections and now you've come back for more? Get out!"

"Mr. Alveston has asked David . . . ," began Terry.

"I won't have it!" bawled Sis. Once again she began making bizarre strokes in the air in her desire to get her hands on David and tear him to pieces.

". . . asked David to bring him a photograph album from the apartment," finished Terry firmly.

"If you think that child is setting a foot in here . . ."

"It's all right, Sis, calm down," said Alison.

"I'm not a social worker; I don't have to just stand by and watch while this horrible little psychopath tries to ruin a decent old man's life by—"

"It's all right, Sis, I'll handle it." Alison turned to Terry. "I'm afraid I can't let you take anything away, not without written permission."

"He *told* me to," said David.

Terry nodded. "He asked him. He wants to look at something."

Alison sighed. She was aware of Sis glowering behind her like the Third Reich. "I'm sorry, you can't take anything. I'll tell you what I will do, though. Tell me what it is you want and I'll give it to Mr. Alveston." She raised her voice for Sis's benefit. "If he wants to show it to you, then that's up to him, I guess."

"He shouldn't be allowed in the hospital," hissed Sis. "He should be IN PRISON. With the other CRIMINALS!"

David felt like hiding behind his dad, but he stood his ground and explained that it was a photograph album, about eight and a half by eleven, with a faded red cover. Then he made a run for it.

Terry lingered. "David said he didn't do it, and I believe him," he said defiantly. "He likes the old man."

"You'll believe bloody anything, then," said Sis. "If he didn't do it himself, he knows who did. You're not trying to tell me it's a coincidence, are you? You're not going to tell me that a completely separate bunch of thugs ended up in the very same apartment and wrecked it just by chance, are you? Because if you are, you must be even more stupid than you look." She turned away and lifted a tangled mass of smashed picture frame and glass in the air.

Terry shrugged. "It wasn't David," he said again. Then he beat it, too. All he knew was David said he hadn't done it, and Mr. Alveston said David hadn't done it, and this wasn't the time to disbelieve either of them. But he wasn't entirely sure he believed them, either.

Mr. Alveston hadn't suffered any serious injuries. There were no broken bones or anything like that. He was badly shaken up and bruised, but nothing worse, and it looked as though he'd be back and up on his feet in a week or so. But it didn't work out like that.

Overnight, he developed a lung infection. It all happened so fast. By the next day he had full-blown pneumonia. Suddenly it was in the cards that he might not survive to the end of the week.

David couldn't believe it. When he'd visited him the day after he went into the hospital, Mr. Alveston had been pale, but he didn't look all that ill. David had brought grapes and large-print books to read from the library—Mr. Alveston had trouble with small print. They'd had a lively conversation about the ghost boy and what he'd done, and what it all meant. Mr. Alveston was certain he knew the ghost—or used to—but he couldn't for the life of him remember who it was.

"I *did* know, I'm sure of it. That face used to be as familiar to me as my own. But it's gone—completely gone! Now isn't that strange?"

That's when the old man had asked David to fetch the photo album from his apartment. He was certain that there was a picture of the boy in there. Maybe there'd even be a name. But when David came back the next day to see if Alison had delivered the album, Mr. Alveston was so ill, he wasn't allowed in to see him.

At first, no one would tell him what was going on. David had to get his dad to call. Mr. Alveston was in intensive care.

"Pneumonia is very serious when you get that old. He might not make it," said Terry. "There's nothing we can do."

As if that wasn't bad enough, the police were back on David's doorstep. This time the problem was far more serious. It was a policewoman this time—much nicer than the last one, or so she seemed. She wanted to know where David had been when the apartment was being wrecked.

"He was at home with me when we got the call," said Terry quickly.

"I didn't do it this time," insisted David. "Mr. Alveston's told you that, hasn't he? He saw someone else."

"Yes, he has told us that; we know there was another boy in there. But we don't know whether he was alone or not, David. Judging by the mess in there, it looks as though there was more than one person."

So that was it! They thought David had been there too, hiding.

"The door was locked," went on the policewoman. "The ducts in there are blocked up. Whoever did it must have locked the door from the outside after they'd finished it. We know there's a key been kept here with your dad, David. Do you know anyone else who has a key?"

David licked his lips. "I don't know," he said. And he could see right then that no one was going to believe him.

"Think," said the policewoman coolly.

But what could he say? He couldn't explain about the ghost. Who on earth would believe that? This time, it was all so much worse. As the policewoman pointed out, the old man might die as a result of his fall. There was a word for this crime. The word was *manslaughter.* It was just a couple of steps down from murder.

David spent the next week in a state of shock. So did Terry. He was used to David being in trouble, but this was different. He spoke to the police and to Alison Grey. Alison was reassuring.

"Mr. Alveston said he saw someone and it wasn't David," she said. "The police have taken finger-prints and searched the apartment. If David's telling the truth, he has nothing to worry about. But it would help if they could catch this lad."

David thought there wasn't much chance of that. It would be the first ghost to be arrested in police history. If Mr. Alveston did die, who would defend him then?

The week dragged on and on and on. Terry called the hospital every evening. Early in the week Mr. Alveston was in a "critical condition." A couple of days later he was "resting comfortably," and they thought he was going to get better, but the next night he was in a "critical condition" again and David was certain he'd never see him again. But then he was "resting," and then he was making a "steady recovery." Finally he had "turned the corner" and the worst was over. He was going to make it. It had been ten days since David had first visited him in the hospital before he was allowed back in to see him.

Mr. Alveston lay on his pillows like a scrap of meat. Small though he was, he looked somehow as if his whole body was too big for him to move. Everything was so slow. When he moved his eyes to look at David, they seemed to float slowly across. He lifted his head like a tortoise. He was like something that had begun a long, long time ago and was running out of strength and time.

He greeted David and Terry with a smile and patted the edge of the bed to show David where to sit. Terry stood by the bedside and smiled uncertainly at him.

"It's good to see you," he said. "We thought we were going to lose you for a while there."

Mr. Alveston smiled and lifted a frail hand in the air. "I want to go," he whispered. "I want so much to go, but I can't."

Terry made a sympathetic face and glanced at David anxiously. Talking about wanting to die in front of his son worried him.

"Now." Mr. Alveston patted David's hand where it rested on the covers. "The book. I expect you must have been worried that you would never find out. It's on my shelf. Go on, fetch it."

David leaned over to the shelf next to the bed and soon found the red-bound book that Alison Grey had given to Mr. Alveston.

"On the fourth page. You'll see him. You'll know him."

David opened the book on the fourth page—and out of the page there looked back at him the face of the ghost. The photo was in black and white, it was old and faded somewhat, but perfectly clear. The boy was standing against a brick wall, holding one wrist in the other hand, staring at the camera. His hair was short at the sides and with a curly mop at the front. He was wearing a sleeveless sweater, a shirt rolled up at the sleeves, and short trousers that came down to his knees. He looked out across the years with a serious face, slightly lowered, as if the camera made him anxious. His long face, the slight bags under his eyes, the large, square teeth—it was him, all right: the boy who had become a ghost.

"That's him, isn't it?" asked Mr. Alveston.

"Yes, that's him. Who is it?"

"I haven't got the slightest clue."

"You must know!"

"I *should* know. I'm sure I used to know, but I don't now. It's gone. Let me tell you something. I have—I used to have—a marvelous memory. Everybody said so. Not for where I put things, or names or dates, or that sort of thing. For people. I never forget a face. But when I try to think of this face, I get nothing. Just a blank." Mr. Alveston looked down at the page. "It's as if something has been taken away from me."

"Excuse me, but is there something I don't know?" asked Terry. He had no idea what this conversation was all about.

Mr. Alveston smiled and looked up at him. "Yes, your poor father, he hasn't got a clue what we're talking about. Well, you see, Terry, we've seen a ghost. Yes, yes, you heard me correctly. A ghost. David saw it when he was playing in the ventilation system. I saw it, too. It was the ghost who wrecked my apartment. Ah, now, I see you don't believe me. Well, why should you? You are very much of this world. Sometimes the young and the old see things that people in the middle can't understand. I assure you, every word I say is true. Yes." He laughed at the expression on Terry's face. "I'm an old man at the very end of my life. Why should I make it up?"

"Of course, if you say so," said Terry. But he was really thinking something very serious. He was thinking that if this poor old man thought it was a ghost that had wrecked his apartment, there was no way on earth that the police were going to believe him when he said it wasn't David who did it.

"Seeing a ghost isn't so unusual. But in this case there is a problem, for me. I feel sure that it is this ghost *who is keeping me here in this world.* I have come a very long way. There is a door just out of reach that I have to go through to leave this life, and this boy—this ghost—is standing between me and that door. I want so very much to be able to get there. Do you understand? Going through that door is the last task of my life and he won't let me do it."

Mr. Alveston had been talking eagerly, but now his head lay back on the pillow and he closed his eyes. Just that short talk had exhausted him.

"Look—we're scaring your father." He smiled in amusement. "Poor Terry!" Mr. Alveston beckoned them to come close so that he could speak in a whisper.

"I want to ask you a favor, both of you. I want you to find out who the boy in that photograph is. Look in my other photograph albums. I have many photographs. Maybe you can find his name. I have to know who he is. . . ."

"I promise," said David. "But you'll have to tell

them to let us in. They wouldn't let us near your things last time."

Mr. Alveston nodded.

"I'll help," said Terry, although he didn't believe a word of it. "But can I ask one thing?" The old man lifted his hand to say, Ask away. "You know that the police think it might be David who did this to your apartment."

"Of course it wasn't David . . ."

"It's just that—maybe it isn't such a good idea to tell them that this boy you saw—that it was a ghost . . ."

"Tell the police about a ghost? Oh, no. I'm not stupid. Of course I won't do that. No, don't worry. I'll tell them . . . a good story."

Terry smiled. Mr. Alveston had his lapses, but when he was on the ball, he was as sharp as a nail. "It's a deal," he said. "I'll help."

Mr. Alveston needed to rest. He told David to take the photo out of the album, and then they said good-bye and left.

At the hospital door, Terry told David to go and wait by the car. "I want to have a word with the nurse," he told him.

"Why can't I come?"

"They don't always tell everything when there's a

child there," said Terry. He wanted to ask how Mr. Alveston was doing.

The nurse shook her head. "He could pop off at any time," she said. "To be honest, I think that's what he wants. All we can do is keep him comfortable. He isn't in any pain, I don't think," she added, to try and make Terry feel better about it. Terry nodded, but that wasn't what scared him. He was worried about David. He wondered if he ought to tell him that the old man was going to die.

And he was scared his son was going to end up in prison.

Terry didn't believe in ghosts, but he was a man of his word as far as he was able. When he got home, he got right to work with carrying out his promise and gave Alison Grey a ring. He told her about Mr. Alveston wanting to find out who the boy in the photograph was. He didn't tell her about the ghost, of course, or the strange story about the boy stopping the old man from leaving this world. He just said it was a memory Mr. Alveston was having trouble with.

Alison said she'd see what she could do, but she wasn't sure whether or not to help. She knew how fond Robert Alveston was of David—he'd told her himself. She'd been seeing David at least once a week for a couple of months, and she felt sure that she knew him well enough to say that he was fond of Mr. Alveston, too. And yet it was impossible to think that the latest attack on the old man's apartment had nothing to do with David. It was just too much of a coincidence.

Privately, the police had told her that David was very unlikely to be prosecuted for the attack. Apart from Mr. Alveston's evidence that someone else had done it, something had gone wrong with the fingerprint tests. The whole apartment had been covered in child-sized fingerprints, which they were sure were going to be David's. But when they looked closely at them, they found that they weren't. In fact, they were like miniature versions of Mr. Alveston's. Of course, that was impossible. Something must have gone wrong with the tests. There were a few of David's, too, but all the evidence showed that his had been made before the apartment had been wrecked. That meant there was no real evidence, and there was nothing to do but let the case drop.

"That doesn't mean he didn't do it," the inspector told Alison. "It just means we can't prove it."

Sis thought the very worst of David, too. "He wants to look through Mr. Alveston's things so he can steal something," she said when Alison told her about David's request to look for the photo. "That's why they wrecked the joint—pulling it to pieces hunting for valuables."

Alison sighed. "But Mr. Alveston is so fond of him. What can I do?"

"That boy has taken advantage of him."

"Mr. Alveston isn't stupid," pointed out Alison. "He's as bright as you like on a good day."

"Yes, well, there's not many of those at the moment, are there?" said Sis.

It was true. Mr. Alveston had recovered from the pneumonia, but it had left him trapped in a strange world in between life and death. He spent a lot of time asleep, but it was not an easy sleep. He seemed no longer to be able to tell the difference between past and present. It was often difficult to tell if he was talking to you, or if a memory had taken over his mind so vividly that it had blotted out the here and now. Yet when he did know what was going on around him, he was frighteningly clear.

"He told me the other day that it was like being lost in a huge maze filled with the past and present all jumbled up together," said Sis. "He said it was like wandering up and down and to and fro, trying to find the way back to the present. And then he said"—and Sis lowered her voice, because what he had said scared her—"then he said that the present was getting harder and harder to find."

"It's the oddest case I've ever come across," said Alison. "I've never known anyone able to think about what's happening to them so clearly."

"Have you noticed how troubled he gets about his childhood?" asked Sis. "I was visiting him the other day and he woke up, looked at me, and said, 'I've lost it, Sis.' And when I asked him what he'd lost, he said, 'My childhood. I've lost it.' "

Alison rubbed her face uncomfortably. "Maybe that's why he wants David to find out who that boy is."

Sis had to admit that he had asked her if David had found out who it was in the photograph yet.

"It does seem to be rather important to him," said Alison, and Sis had to agree that was right.

For another few days, Alison put David and Terry off, not sure what was the best thing to do. Then Terry gave her another call, suggesting that if she didn't trust David enough, maybe she herself could bring the albums by. Two days later she appeared at the door, to David's joy, with a great heap of books in her arms over half a yard high.

"It seems Mr. Alveston took a lot of photos," she said.

The albums were filled with people. It was amazing that Mr. Alveston should have had such a full life yet ended up so alone. Terry made some tea

141

and brought out a plateful of biscuits, and they sat down around the table to flip through the albums. It was a long job. Time after time someone thought they had found the boy in the photograph, and time after time it turned out not to be. There were just so many pictures of people who looked a bit like him, but not quite enough.

"It must be a relative," said Alison, warming to the hunt.

One after the other the old books were opened, examined, and put to one side. It wasn't until they were in the very oldest book, the one that went right back to the few faded pictures of when Mr. Alveston himself had been a child, that they had any success.

It was Terry who found him. "I've got him!" he exclaimed. David peered across—and there he was, the boy who had become a ghost, standing next to a little girl sitting in a little cart. They were both staring at the camera, and they were both smiling—the boy, shyly, but the girl with her face lifted up in delight.

"Is there a name?" asked Alison. Terry pried the picture out of its place, but on the back there was nothing.

They had another picture, but it told them nothing. The search went on.

By the end of the evening they had no less than five pictures of the boy, and they still hadn't solved the mystery. But then they hit the jackpot. David spotted the face this time. It was in a photograph that they'd overlooked several times because it was in a group, and the face was too small to see well.

It was a family picture, two adults in deck chairs on the beach with their children around them. The boy was kneeling on the ground with his arms folded, scowling at the camera this time. There were four other children—two older boys standing to the side, a girl sitting in the sand, and a baby on the mother's knee. The names were written on the back: Charlie, Thomas, Eric, Ellen, Helen, Robert, and Owen. But which name belonged to whom?

"Charlie, Thomas, Eric, Robert, or Owen?" asked Terry. "Which one?"

Alison peered closely at the photo. "Robert," she said. "Robert. That's his name."

"Whose?"

"Mr. Alveston's. Robert. That's his name. Oh my God!" Alison's hand flew up to her mouth. "It can't be, can it? Oh my God, that's spooky!"

But it was. They looked at other photographs of Mr. Alveston at various times of his life. Now that he was an old, old man, the resemblance was not so clear, but when he was younger, you could see it

143

perfectly. It was the same face, all right. Mr. Alveston himself was the ghost.

Alison began to weep. She lifted a tissue to her eye. "Forgetting your own childhood," she wept. "That's just so sad." Then she lifted her face up again. "And he said! He said he'd lost his childhood. He knew. He knew."

And all three of them sitting there felt the mystery of it prickle down their backs.

13

The Ghost and
Mr. Alveston

There are unknown things in this world. David had stumbled across one of them.

Slowly, it began to make a kind of sense. It was Mr. Alveston himself who had said that ghosts might be memories. If anything, wasn't it more likely that a ghost might be a living person's memory rather than the spirit of a dead one? At least memories were still alive.

Inside Mr. Alveston were the memories of all his past lives, and one of them had got out and walked off. The child in him had run away. He had lost his memory in a way no one could have dreamed, and now his ghost was on the loose. No wonder the boy felt so lost. No wonder he was so scared of the old man. No wonder he was keeping him in this world. When Mr. Alveston died, the ghost would die, too.

The boy had already had his turn to be alive, but he didn't know that. He was lost, lost in the endless ductwork behind the walls of Mahogany Villas, and he had no way of finding his way out. What would happen if the old man died before the ghost was back where it belonged? Would it be doomed to live forever like a shadow behind the walls? What if Mr. Alveston couldn't die unless his ghost was back inside him? Would he lie there forever in his hospital bed until he turned to dust and bones?

David knew at once that for both their sakes—for Robert Alveston the old man and Robert Alveston the boy—ghost and man had to get back together again. And who was going to help them do that?

David should have gone in straightaway to tell Mr. Alveston what was going on, but he didn't. He dreaded telling him. Alison visited the old man the day after, though, and on the way home, she called on David with a message. The old man had been amazed, fascinated, appalled when she told who it was in the photograph. He begged David to come and see him as soon as he could.

"That's all right, he can go down this evening," Terry said. David did as he was told, but when he got to the hospital, he couldn't bring himself to go in. He wandered around a bit and stared at the silent windows staring back at him, and went away without going in.

Mr. Alveston couldn't get up to go and get the ghost, so the ghost would have to be brought to Mr. Alveston. But who else knew the ghost? Who else was small enough to go into the ducts to get him out? David knew exactly why Mr. Alveston wanted to see him, and he didn't like it one little bit.

The ghost was dangerous. Each time David had gone into the ducts, it had been worse. The last time the ghost had tried to stop him from getting away by grabbing him by the ankle and David wasn't sure he would have escaped if he hadn't fallen down the duct. Suppose the ghost decided to keep him in there forever? He was lost and lonely; he wanted a friend. If David were to die in the ducts, then the ghost would have a friend, all right—a friend who would never go away, a friend who would stay with him forever. Then there would be two ghosts in Mahogany Villas. Mr. Alveston would never die, but he would continue to get older and older and older, and David himself would be trapped forever behind the walls in the dark, tight ducts.

Oh, no. David was happy with the ducts bricked up and the darkness locked away out of sight. But what about Mr. Alveston? And what about the poor ghost?

A week went by. David wondered who he could turn to for help, but there was no one. Who would believe him? He could hardly believe it himself. He was hoping that Mr. Alveston was going to leave this world all on his own, as he so much wanted to, but each day found the old man still hanging on. The doctors and nurses shook their heads and marveled at how tightly the spirit hung on to life and expected him to be gone in the morning. But the morning came and there he was, pale and still and gray and tired on the pillows, waiting for David to come and visit him.

"I can't believe you!" hissed Terry when he found out. "Over a week gone by! Messages *begging* you to come practically every day and you still haven't been! How could you? After all the trouble you've caused him and all the help he's given you! How *could* you?"

"It's not a visit from *me* he's waiting for," muttered David, half to himself. But his dad was too busy stopping his allowance, banning his TV watching, and grounding him for weeks ahead to even listen.

"And if you aren't there tonight, I'll strangle you.

148

Personally. With these bare hands!" Terry flexed his pale white optician's hands under his son's disgusted nose and stamped off into the kitchen to cook dinner.

No way was David going back into those ducts, whatever Mr. Alveston said to him. But maybe he could just get close to a grille and have a quiet word. . . .

The only trouble was, where? The grilles in his apartment had been bricked up. The hall outside was too public. But there was somewhere David knew of where he could get close up without being seen.

Not all the apartments in Mahogany Villas were occupied. Some of them had been empty for so long and were so run-down that no one wanted to spend the money needed to fix them. They were all boarded up, but from time to time people would break in—homeless people looking for a place to spend the night under a roof when the weather was cold, kids looking for somewhere to hang out or who just kicked the door down for something to do.

There were such apartments on the third floor.

David got home early the next day and rode the elevator up to have a look. Sure enough, there was a door open halfway down the hall. Darkness showed inside. Cautiously, he crept up and looked in. It was a disaster in there. David could see a bed of blankets on the floor and the remains of a fire in a bucket. There were beer cans and litter scattered everywhere. There was a bunch of plastic flowers on top of a cardboard box and on the wall someone had drawn a picture of a dragon in red, yellow, and blue chalk. It stank of soot, stale beer, stale bodies, and urine. The dragon spread his wings over it all. There seemed to be no one at home, though.

David put his ear to the wall under the vent, but he heard nothing. He found an old chair and dragged it to the wall and climbed up. There was no grille in the way; the black insides of the building hung like a mouth in the wall. Before he looked inside, David found himself glancing over his shoulder. What if the ghost had escaped? What if he was haunting this apartment right now?

There was nothing to be seen. David put his head inside the wall.

It was like putting your head inside a gigantic shell. Could he hear voices from far inside or the sound of the ghost moving closer? In this strange world, he couldn't be sure of anything, except for one thing. He didn't want to be doing this.

"Hello?" he called softly. "Hello? Are you there? Can you hear me?" But there was no reply.

For a long, long time David stood on the chair

with his head in the duct. He told himself that if he heard so much as a whisper, he'd take his head out and never come back again. But in the end he did what all the time he knew he had to do. He crawled inside and began to make his way up toward the ghost.

It felt tight in there. His dad was always saying, "You've grown," but this time it was true and David was scared that he might get stuck. Wouldn't that make the ghost happy! Just the thought made him shiver from head to foot. He stopped, thought about backing out. But now that he was in, he was determined to finish it, one way or another. He carried on crawling deep inside.

Soon he came to the big up duct. Now he had to climb two floors up to where Mr. Alveston's apartment was. He shone his flashlight up there, but he couldn't see far—the beam stopped against the piece of wood he had put over the duct. It must have fallen back into place after the janitor knocked it.

But when he shone his flashlight down, the beam fell straight into the terrible drop, all the way to the basement. There was nothing to stop him falling from here.

David paused. He ought to get out. He ought to get another piece of board or find a way in on his own floor, where the drop was already covered over. But it was too late now. He was on his way. If he left now, he might never come back.

David wedged the flashlight into his jeans, worked his way carefully into the big duct, trying not to think of the deadly drop directly underneath him, and began to push his way up. He'd gone no more than a couple of yards when there was a sudden noise above his head. With a thrill of pure fear, David looked up. The board above him disappeared with a loud click—and suddenly, without any more warning than that, he was staring straight into the face of the ghost.

David was so scared, wedged there helplessly in the duct with the ghost above him and a fall nearly five floors down underneath him, that he couldn't even think, let alone speak. He could hear the board banging and booming as it was blown down the ducts, deeper into the heart of the building. Lit by the eerie glow of his flashlight that twisted and bounced off the dull metal of the ducts, the ghost's face seemed at one moment miles away, at the next so close, it could lean forward and bite him. He could see the little teeth glinting like shiny stones in his mouth.

"You left me," hissed the ghost. "In the dark! You left me all on my own."

David swallowed and tried to get his voice back. What could he say? He opened his mouth and the word came out without him even thinking.

"Robert," he said.

"No!" screamed the ghost. "No—not me, him! Don't you call me that! Don't you dare call me by *his* name!"

"Robert Alveston," said David, trying to stop his voice from shaking. "That's who you are. Aren't you?"

"You—you—don't you dare!" yelled the ghost, mad with fear and fury. "Don't you call me that! I'll teach you! I'll teach you! You'll never get out of here alive!"

And it came at him like a ton of bricks.

Being a ghost, the boy didn't have to touch him. Instead it forced itself down the duct toward him. There was a sudden gust of wind, and then a hard cold force pressing down on him. David began to slide back down. The ghost was as strong as a machine, and he knew at once that there was nothing he could do about it. He wedged himself as tightly as he could, clenched his teeth, and pressed, but it made no difference at all. He was being blown slowly down the duct like a bubble in a straw. The skin was coming off his hands, he was pressing so hard, but he was wasting his time. In another second he'd be at the junction of the third floor, there would be nothing for him to hold on to, and he would be shot—bang—right down the ducts all the way to the basement and certain death.

"You'll never leave me again!" screamed the ghost, in a terrible fury. "Now you'll find out what it's like to be stuck in here! See how you like it!"

Already David could feel where the duct ended. In desperation he opened his mouth and yelled.

"Don't!" he screamed.

Above him the ghost gasped, and fell. It was as if opening his mouth had opened up a pit underneath it. Still screaming, David closed his eyes and winced. His mouth shut. For a moment he felt the ghost squirming on top of him like an icy hard shadow. Then he opened his mouth to yell again and— pop!—it fell again, right inside him. He could feel it brush past his jaws. With a snap he closed his mouth, bit hard with his teeth . . .

And there was silence.

A second before, the wind had been raging around him, but now everything was still. David hung there a moment longer, poised on the very edge of the drop, wondering what was going to happen next. Nothing did. Ever so slowly, he eased himself out of the duct and lay down on the cross duct, safe at last, gasping for breath through his nose. He kept his mouth shut tight.

For maybe ten minutes David lay there, waiting to see what was coming next. It really seemed as if he'd trapped the ghost inside him. Or perhaps the ghost had taken him over? Which was which? Who was who?

Am I him? thought David. Or is he me?

He had no idea.

Carefully he got up on all fours. He climbed into the duct and began to slide his way down. He had no idea who he was, no idea if it was him or the ghost who crept down and along to the vent on the third floor and got out into the abandoned apart-ment. He brushed his clothes down—or was it the ghost doing that? Then he—or someone who looked like him—walked out of the building and turned down the road toward the hospital.

Was it David going to save the old man—or the ghost going to kill him?

It was the strangest feeling, not knowing if you were yourself or something completely different. Were those his feet pacing one in front of the other, or were they the ghost's feet? What was the difference between them, now that they were the same per-son? And as he looked at all the people and things in the streets around him—the cars, the shops and houses, the people hurrying to and fro—David began to feel that maybe he wasn't anything at all. What was the difference between him and all this around him, after all? What was it that made him himself, separate and alone? He stopped and stared at the stone beneath his feet. He wondered if maybe he was that stone, and that being David Withington was just a dream. Am I looking at it, or is David looking at me? he thought. But then he shook his head and walked on, frightened that just thinking such things would stop him from being himself ever again—that at any moment he would turn into the ghost, or a paving stone or a brick in the wall, and David Withington would disappear forever.

In the hospital, visiting time was coming to an end. Sis Parkinson was talking to one of the nurses. She'd just been in to see Mr. Alveston.

He'd been having one of his better days, but the old man was just a shadow of what he had been. The really sad thing, which upset Sis more than anything, was the way he was just hanging on without wanting to. He had said to her more times than she could count that he just wanted to let go and die.

"You can't blame him," said Sis. "God help us all to know when it's time for us to go. But then there's no one there to help you find the way!"

"And there's no one ever came back to tell you

how to do it, did they? It's a shame. We're not allowed to help people pass away. Our job is to help them stay alive," said the nurse. "All we can do is make him comfortable and let him get on with it. Everyone was expecting him to go weeks ago, but he just can't seem to take the final few steps."

Sis nodded. It was at that moment that she caught sight of that brat, David Withington from Mahogany Villas, marching down the corridor with a cool look in his eye, straight for the old man's room. He spotted her glaring at him and did a quick little dash into Mr. Alveston's room before she could say anything.

"Look at that! Bold as brass. Visiting hours are over. I'll throw him out for you—let the poor old thing rest in peace," she snapped. But the nurse stopped her.

"He likes the lad; let them have five minutes together," she said.

Sis snorted in disgust. "I wouldn't let him in here if I had my way. People are too soft on that boy," she said. She looked over at the door. "He could be doing anything. Stealing his fruit. Or his medication. It wouldn't surprise me. That child is capable of anything!"

Inside the room, David was standing in front of the bed, smiling shyly. The old man turned his slow head on the pillow and smiled back. For the first time since he had left home, David opened his mouth.

"Hello, I'm sorry I was so long," he said. As he spoke, he heard two voices saying the same thing, and there was the ghost standing beside him, staring at the old man.

Mr. Alveston smiled, but he didn't seem to know which was the ghost and which was David. "Yes, yes, I knew you'd come back home," he said. The ghost tried to turn his face away to look at David, but he seemed unable to look away from the old man. Mr. Alveston patted the bed next to him.

"Sit down, sit with me," he said. "You know we belong together, don't you?"

The ghost, quite clear now, a pale boy of eight or nine years, took a few uncertain steps across the room and sat down where the old man had told him.

"Now, then," said Mr. Alveston. He put his hand on the boy's hand. The ghost turned to look at David, and David smiled at him. He looked calm now. Quietly, he lay down on the bed next to Mr. Alveston, and before David's eyes, he began to fade away. He lay quite still and simply melted away. It happened quickly, no longer than a minute. When he had gone completely, Mr. Alveston smiled like an angel.

"Now I remember *everything*," he said.

"It was you, wasn't it?" asked David.

"It was me, all the time." Mr. Alveston looked vaguely at him and gave a wondering shake of his head. Then, silently and easily, he relaxed into the pillow and fell asleep.

David stood for a while, watching the old man's chest rise and fall, rise and fall. He knew that he was never going to wake up. Standing there by the bed, he burst suddenly into tears. But whether they were tears for himself, or for the boy or for Mr. Alveston, he could not say.

Glossary

biscuit. Cookie.

cheeky. Naughty.

fish-and-chips. Fried fish and french fries.

Great War. World War I, 1914–18.

skip. Dumpster.

skive off. To evade doing one's task or duty.

sod that. An exclamation of contempt or frustration.

spanner in the works. Wrench in the machine; delay or problem.

Third Reich. The empire of Adolf Hitler during World War II, 1939–45.

tube. The British underground system of trains, or subways.

twenty-pound note. A piece of British paper currency.

About the Author

Melvin Burgess says, "I was an extremely dreamy and shy child, and I used to wander around muttering to myself and playing games with imaginary friends. My parents had to shout, 'He's in the land!' to explain to people why I apparently couldn't hear what they were saying. I did very badly at school— I was daydreaming too much to concentrate on anything much. It wasn't until I was pretty nearly grown up that I started to think that the world around me might be at least as interesting as what was going on in my head."

After training as a journalist, Melvin decided that

what he really wanted to do was write fiction. For the next fifteen years he wrote on and off, but it wasn't until he was in his thirties that he decided to see if he could make a living at it. His first novel, *The Cry of the Wolf,* was short-listed for the Carnegie Medal.

He has been writing award-winning books ever since.